THE THIRD UNIVERSAL EVENT HORIZON

BY

JOSEPH A. WAILES

OUTLAW PRESS
RAWHIDE, TEXAS

ISBN 978-0-9916454-5-9
PRINTED AND BOUND IN
THE UNITED STATES OF AMERICA

OUTLAW PRESS
2980 PHYLLIS LANE
RAWHIDE, TEXAS
75234-6425

THE WINNER OF THE HUMAN RACE

BY
JOSEPH A. WAILES

I_WHEN LIGHT BECAME A MAN

II_THE LONGEST NIGHT

III_ANCIENT DREAMS,
NEWBORN VISIONS

IV_WAR OF THE BOOK

V_THE THIRD UNIVERSAL
EVENT HORIZON

VI_HARVEST MOON

VII_TOO GOOD TO BE UNTRUE

BOOKS AVAILABLE AT OUTLAW PRESS

TABLE OF CONTENTS

FOREWORD

Some of my readers have asked me, "Is that in the Bible?" While most of my reference material is indeed, found in Scripture, there are other sources as well, only included if they are not contradictory to the Scripture.

The dreams and visions, which were granted unto me, also have been a major source of a lot of the ideas. I just have to trust that the good Lord has been the source of the fine dreams and visions, and I have merely done my best effort to accurately describe what I was shown.

I have tried to stress a few major points. There is only One God. He is a good God. He cares about us. He intends good things for us. There is only One Creator, and only one creation, not a multitude of alternate universes. God does not need second chances, since He always does everything right, the first time He tries.

Life with the good Lord is full, but trying to live without Him is futile. Come on with us, and find out just how exciting life with King Jesus can be! (I warn you, it can be a rough road, but worth the effort, indeed!)

REGENERATION

The most massive project in human history was already underway. Various quick strategy and planning sessions had lasted long into the night, for over a week, and then leaders had been assigned, and then special teams, hand-picked, and then assembled, and then trained into well-coordinated units. Each particular segment of the entire task force had its' own individual responsibilities. There were teams to work on land projects, and also teams to work on ocean projects. They even had very specialized teams to work on atmospheric projects. Space was not a super priority at the moment, since more urgent matters required action, immediately.

The two men pulled off to one side of the road, and stopped the jeep. As the desert dust swirled around them, and then blew away, they killed the engine, and climbed out. They were clad in special radiation protection, from head to toe, including respirators. The desert dust still looked the same, and blew around the same, as it had done for millions of years. These days, it was miserably fatal to breathe it into one's lungs.

Off road vehicles had become the only ones practical, since the shattering earthquakes, which had been triggered by the monster impact of the huge asteroid Ceres. When it had hit, on the Pacific Ocean side of Earth, the heavy shockwaves caused by a 600-mile in diameter mountain of solid rock had splintered the whole surface of the planet into many new tectonic plates. After the impact of an earlier hard hit from a tiny dark star (only a few miles in radius, but still more massive, by far, than Ceres), the Earth's original tectonic layer, at first a solid shell, had splintered apart into fourteen major plates. After Ceres hit, the total number of plates increased to 42.

The result of the first hit was that Pangaea had become many continents, instead of just one giant one, and the Earth began to manifest all four seasons, in all the weather and long term climate patterns, instead of just monsoon, and drought, endlessly repeated. Mountain ranges formed, ice ages happened, with glaciers, and time began to carve new things into the surface of Earth.

The result of the second impact, the one of Ceres, was that all of the railroad tracks, and all of the paved roads, all over the world, had shattered into millions of fragments. All large paved areas suffered the same destruction, as did all large buildings in cities. Some mountains of solid granite had even split asunder, and the initial shockwave had even slightly moved every single mountain in the world a fraction of an inch out of place. Many more new, smaller continents could form over the eons ahead, and weather patterns could change more, and the grand diversity of the living creatures upon Earth could be able to increase even further over times ahead.

There were other hard shocks that had also hit the Earth. Some of them had even been made by men, such as the nuclear detonations. Many had happened deliberately near Israel. Much of that had even occurred in connection with the final grand battle at the Valley of Megiddo. The dead bodies of the fallen armies of the world had taken months to finally remove, and burn. When the number of the dead corpses is about a half a billion, it is not a five minute job to clean up. The sterilization process was still not yet complete, a full two years now since the return of King Jesus Christ.

The two Hebrew soldiers, in radiation suits, were following a small but advanced Geiger counter needle, as it led them straight to another dead body, hidden in the radioactive sand. As one of them took a standard entrenching tool, and scraped away the sand and dirt from the remains, the other one took out a special, heavy-gauge, lead-shielded body bag, and unzipped the lockable zipper. As they loaded the bag, they noticed that the guy was still wearing the ragged remnants of a Russian uniform. Perhaps he had been a Muslim radical from Chechnya. Maybe he had just been another Russian soldier, since they had brought their entire army to the fight. Either way, now he was just a bunch of radioactive trash, which needed to be removed.

As the men worked, they talked. The younger one said, "I still do not understand why He cannot just speak the command, and force all things to snap back to the way they were when He first made them all, in the days of the Garden of Eden."

The older one smiled a hidden smile inside his mask, and slightly shook his head, and said, "That's not the Way that

He wants to do it this time around. He wants to give us the honor of helping Him to achieve it."

The younger one said, "Well, okay, I can see that. Does that mean we could not have about a dozen good angels out here helping us to finish this loathsome task? After all, they could see them, through the dirt, and round them all up, all over Israel, in less than a day!"

The older one sighed, and said, "You know very well that the good angels are with the good cherubs, working on the really big projects, which no machinery of mankind can accomplish. Right now, they are repairing the gigantic hole bored into the Earth, and also working deep inside the planet, to restore normal structural stability there, once more, so we can start to build buildings again, without the constant threat of earthquakes, anywhere, anytime."

The younger one barked a dry laugh, and said, "Yes, it will be good to dwell in something beyond a tent, once again, even if our people are historically nomadic!"

The older one thought a second or two, and then said, "Besides, if He were to just command all things to return to their original state, which we know He surely could easily perform, and they would instantly obey His direct order, and return, then what ever gain has been won since the Garden, by the hard trials and ordeals of all of humanity, including even our good King, Jesus Christ, could not ever have happened. It had to be done just this Way, and no other. There is no other way in which all of God's prophecies, which could never be broken, could have ever been fulfilled!"

As they carried the bag, and contents, back to the jeep, the older one said, "Come on. Let's head back. In another hour they are scheduled to send crop dusters over this entire area. It's too hard to see to drive through that black dust, once they get started."

They climbed back in, started the jeep, and headed back toward town. The black dust had not yet started falling from the sky. Even though it looked evil, and very deadly, it was actually the healing antidote to neutralize the deadliness of the dust of the Earth. The black dust was made of the same carbon which was used for control rods, in a nuclear reactor. It absorbed radiation, and accelerated the decay rate, by drastically shortening the effective half-life of the active elements nearby. Instead of taking thousands of years, before all of Israel would once again be a lush garden, the process would be completed in about nine hundred years, instead. Israel would enjoy the last century of the Millennium, having been once again restored to the former abundance, which God had once given them, and now, to even greater glory.

Restoring the whole earth to wholeness again was not a short term adventure, even though it would eventually be done. The most massive project in human history was already underway.

A NEW HEAVEN AND A NEW EARTH

Altogether, there were 1.4 billion of them, and all of them were on the move. For a solid year now, they had been steadily gathering here from the farthest reaches of the Earth. For a remarkably busy period of five years, the human race had been scattered all around the face of the planet, each group and individual working and fulfilling every task and project that had been assigned unto them all by the King of Kings, in Person.

There was considerable damage to repair, and restoration and upgrades to perform, and new designs and systems to install and calibrate. The oceans were a wreck, as were the land masses, and the rivers had all been so ruined with poisons that nothing could live in them, or drink the water. One of the first major projects had been the installation of solar powered water pumping and purification stations, scattered at all strategic locations, such as along roadways, and near population centers. The resurrected sons and daughters of light could not die, but every living thing with a flesh body still needed and craved a cool drink of water, on a hot summer's day. Meanwhile, enormous reactor powered monster-sized and capacity water purification systems were being built and installed, at every fresh water reservoir and lake in the world, and even larger purifiers, which were powered by a new design of super reactor, driven by argon plasma, in a tightly controlled flow, that produced an operating temperature of over a million degrees. The reactors themselves were positioned in Earth-synchronous orbits, at 300 miles up, and the power generated there was beamed down to large collector dishes along the shore, which each powered in turn a city sized water purification factory. All of the remaining planned plants should be installed and running in another fifteen years, and, after that, about a century of work would restore the oceans to the original condition, as they were at the time of the Garden of Eden.

Similar efforts and improvements were also underway in the atmosphere, which had already cleared almost back to normal, since the total volume of air could be filtered and cleaned much faster than the total volume of ocean. The air moved through filtration machines faster as a gas, than water as a liquid.

The land was also being cleaned out and restored, even of nuclear debris. That was some of the nastiest and most unpleasant work. The dirt still held too many ugly dead secrets, even five years after the return of King Jesus.

Men were not alone in their efforts. The three good cherubs, and all of the good angels, now that war was only history, had been eager to join in the restoration work, and to help in doing the things that even most of the resurrected sons and daughters of light could not do. These days, all humans and all angels were mighty, and they all were good, too. Not all humans had been granted the same strength the first time they had lived, and the same thing applied now, in their second lifetimes. A small percentage of the humans were even stronger than the three cherubs, which had always been the strongest of all created beings, second in power only to the good Lord Himself. Now, some humans had been given so much strength, from the Lord, Himself, that the cherubs, even all three of them at once, would have been no match for one of the mightiest humans, those closest unto the Lord Jesus Christ.

At the very beginning of the sixth year, at high noon, on the day of spring equinox, a great proclamation had been read. A mighty angel had read with a voice like thunder that in a year, all men, everywhere, were required by Royal Order, to be present, no exceptions, no excuses, not even death, within the borders of Israel, no later than sundown in one year, less a day. The next spring equinox eve that rolled around, everyone had better have his human toes inside the borders of Israel, or the angels would go grab him, or her, by the hair, and carry them there immediately.

As the last year had passed, people had mothballed their machines, to prevent rust, and stored what they needed to store, and protected what they needed to protect, and packed some backpacks, and headed from all corners to Jerusalem. They walked, they took boats, staying out of the water, they drove off road vehicles, and they even flew in some of the planes that had been either rebuilt, or built new from scratch. All of the humans and angels had wings, and all of the angels could fly, but not all of the humans had wings that were long enough, or strong enough for them to actually soar like eagles, but some of the mighty humans could, and did.

As sundown began, a great angel blew a huge shofar from the porch of the new Temple, and said, "Now this sundown ends the Year Six of the Millennium, and Year Seven of the Millennium will officially begin at sunrise tomorrow morning. This year shall be a Holy Year of Rest, a Sabbath Year, of thanksgiving and praise, and glory unto our God, Who is the good Lord Jesus Christ! To Him be glory and honor forever!"

As he said this last word, all the angels of Heaven around him in the air said at once, "Baruk!" When they said this, they had flashed into visibility in the darkening evening sky, and then vanished just as suddenly, as the echo of the word faded.

The angel raised his arms, holding the ram's horn, up to Heaven, and shouted, "Light your candles!"

Instantly, all of the 1.4 billion resurrected humans, which were tightly squeezed into the old borders of Israel, lit their candles all over the nation. The whole countryside glittered with candles, and no other light, except the stars, as far as the eye could see, in every direction. The angel had vanished after his last order. Now, even though he remained unseen, the great angel blew another mighty, long note upon the shofar, and then shouted, "Behold the KING!!!"

As he finished, suddenly King Jesus appeared in His full glory, with His great wings outstretched, but motionless. He was suspended, still, in mid air, about a mile above the Temple Mount, and the light coming from Him lit up the whole city like the Sun. As if reading the thoughts of the folks on the ground below, Jesus lowered His level of luminance, and He turned down the bright light some, as one might adjust down a light switch in a room. He kept slowly dimming the glare, until people could once again see both Him, and the stars in the night sky around Him. Even though He was way up in the air, everyone could miraculously see Him clearly, and also, when He began to speak, it was as though He was standing right next to you, and everyone could hear every Word clearly.

As He started, every ear was so eager to hear, that not a single whisper was heard. Even the crickets were listening.

His first words were a little surprising. He suddenly smiled, and the light grew instantly brighter again, as though it could not quite restrain itself, for joy, and excitement, and He shouted to all of them, "Merry Christmas!" He let that sink in for a few seconds, and then went on, "You know that tomorrow is My Birthday, and My re-Birthday, and the first day of Spring, and the first day of Passover. It is also the first day of our first Sabbath Year in our new Earth. We are going to do something special this night, which will be for a memorial for all our hard work, and all of your faith, and all of our faithfulness unto the Father, both in the old world, and now. This is the night of prophecies kept, and blessings fulfilled, and you are witnesses to Creation as it happens, this night, and you will tell your children and grandchildren of this night forever, through all your generations. You have all worked hard, and I am indeed proud of you, My little brothers and sisters, and I have a couple of special presents for you all tonight. Everyone has worked hard, doing the part they could do, and now it is My turn, to do some of what you cannot do. It is a mystery, and a surprise, which I planned for you before the world began, and told you about in the Revelation which I gave unto John.

Now, blow out your candles, and watch the night sky with Me!"

He looked up into the stars, and waited a few seconds, while everyone finished putting out their little candles, and the whole countryside went dark again, except for the dimmed glow of King Jesus, still about a mile up over the Temple.

Suddenly, He shouted, "Venus, come closer! Mars, come meet Venus!"

As the people watched, astonished, with sounds of "ooohs" and "aaahs" all over the nation, and a lot of "Wow!" also, a couple of the unnoticed stars began to move at impossible speeds, growing rapidly much larger, as they came nearer, and began also to close the gap between each other.

As the entire human race stared up, mesmerized, the spectacle happened at fast forward speed, right before their bugged out eyes. If the lights at ground level had not been out, their faces, full of wonder, would have been shown as stunningly beautiful, with joy and delight!

Venus arrived nearby first, since it started closest. Suddenly the Lord shouted, "Close enough, Venus! Hold still, and wait for your hot date. His name is Mars! Here he comes now!"

As Jesus said this, Mars arrived, at ultrasonic speed, and slammed into Venus, like a freight train into a stack of hay bales on the tracks! The blinding explosion and huge eruption and scattering of gas and matter from both planets momentarily obscured precisely what the two planets were doing in there. As the dust cloud began to clear, and started forming a huge ring around everything, it could be seen that the two planets had been permanently fused into one larger new one, surrounded by a nearly solid sphere of rocky dust and excess atmosphere from Venus, which had always had way too much atmosphere, anyway. Venus had been about 0.8 earth masses before, since it had a much smaller iron core than did Earth. Mars had been about 0.6 Earth masses before, being smaller, with almost no iron core by comparison. As a result of the impact, the new planet had shed some of its' total mass, and now was about 1.17 Earth masses, almost precisely the same mass as the total Earth-moon system.

The Lord said, "New planet, I name you Ahava!"

As He said this, all the unseen angels in the night around Him shouted "Baruk!" When they did, they flashed brightly visible in the night, until they finished saying the word, and then they vanished back instantly into the night.

Next, King Jesus looked at another bright speck in the night, and commanded, "Mercury, leave your old friend the Sun, and come here to Me!"

As everyone watched, again amazed, the planet began to move swiftly nearer and grew rapidly much larger. When it was well underway, and about halfway there to them, King Jesus commanded, "Now fly close by the new planet, and scrape all of the excess dust, rocks, and gas that are waiting there in the gas cloud for you to collect, and pass through it three times, so that you collect every bit of it for yourself."

As they watched the live, ultra high speed cosmic events occur before their stunned eyes, the people saw Mercury swing through and collect all of the dust and gas around Ahava, as Mercury's own gravity pulled it all right down on to the surface of Mercury itself. For the first time since the Sun had first lit up, Mercury was growing an atmosphere again. It was not until 2010 that scientists had realized that Mercury was no ordinary planet, but was more like a cannonball the size of a planet. The Earth had a very large iron core, but Mercury was entirely iron core, and not much else. The whole thing was a giant ball of molten iron and other metals, which was never allowed to cool off and truly solidify, because of extreme proximity to the Sun. Of all the planets in the solar system, there was no planet more impossible for life than Mercury. Even though Mercury was much smaller than Earth, physically, it weighed as much as old Venus had, about 0.8 earth masses. After it had collected all of the excess debris from the merger of the planets, it now weighed about 1.16 Earth masses, which was about the same as the Earth-moon system. Now, as the good Lord had planned it, and worked it to come to pass, all three of the planets were almost identical in mass, which made them much easier to balance perfectly.

Then the Lord said, "Okay, well done, planets! Mercury, now I give you a new name, also, for you are now also a new planet! From now on you shall be called Lehaim, for you were the deadest world, and now you will overflow with life!"

Then He raised His great and mighty arms, and said, "I bless you, new planets, which were made this night before the eyes of My brothers and sisters! May you both always be strong, and become safe and comfortable homes for Us, and our pets! Now, take your assigned places, which I ordained before the world began!"

As soon as He had said this, each of the new planets began to shift away from them, into the night, and each one moved into the same precise orbit and speed and direction of travel as the Earth. They latched in at the two orbital balance points in Earth orbit, O-2, and O-3, which locked them tidally in a permanent triangle with the Earth, as all three of them raced around the Sun, forever chasing each other, but never catching up. Earth came first, followed by Ahava, which was followed by Lehaim. The Lord had also caused the tilt axis of each planet to match precisely to Earth's, at 23½ degrees. The rotations were each set to the same as the Earth, so all three planets ended up with the precise same climate, seasons, days and nights, and temperatures, and the gravity fields were precisely the same. Ahava now had a combined iron core similar to Earth's, though smaller, but a significant magnetic field was beginning to form around the planet, which was necessary for radiation shielding, and to help hold the atmosphere stable. Lehaim had a plenty strong enough magnetic field, but it would diminish over time, as the planet finished cooling and setting, and the spinning generator inside began to slow down. For a while, the aurora show around Lehaim was a great spectacle for everyone, every night, especially during a lot of solar activity.

As the planets settled into place, moving, but never moving, at 70,000 miles per hour around the Sun, but at zero miles per hour between each other, they went through the same cycle of seasons, only each one four months apart from the one ahead, and also from the one behind. It was always summer, or late spring, somewhere, from then on forever. It was always also winter, or late autumn, somewhere else, from then on, too.

King Jesus lowered His arms to stretch out over all the people, and blessed them all, just as the very first light of the dawn, of a new year, and of His Birthday, was beginning to glow in the east. He said, "Now, remember forever the night when you saw Me create something brand new, right before your eyes! Go home, get some much deserved rest, take this Sabbath Year off, and we will resume projects again, this time next year. You have all done perfectly well! Now, I will tell you the secret name of your own planet: it is "Shalom". The proper name of My capital city is actually Yeshua-Shalom, the Jesus-peace. My name is Jesus, the planet's name is Peace!"

After a few seconds to let that all sink in, He went on, "I told you that I would make all things new, and that I was going to prepare a place for you, a home with many mansions. I told you that I was going to make you a new Heaven, and a new Earth. This night, this prophecy has been fulfilled in your seeing! Behold! The new Heaven and the new Earth!"

WRITTEN IN THE DUST

Another sixth year was winding down. As soon as the first Sabbath Year had ended, people had resumed their repairs and redesign efforts. The atmosphere was almost normally clean, again, at least back up to 21st Century standards, before all of the destruction had happened. The oceans were taking longer, as were the badly contaminated land regions, wherever the nuclear contamination was worst. The massive works were not confined to only one big planet, anymore, either. Now, there was already much work underway on both Ahava, and also on Lehaim. The two new planets were raw, and still were not habitable for humans, but that was already changing.

In addition to all of the human efforts, angels also were hard at work, doing the heavy lifting things that were either too strenuous or too dangerous for humans to do them. Oddly enough, all of the humans were still growing much stronger, and their powers were increasing, as well, but they were much like infants learning to walk and talk, all over again. Just because you have an indestructible body does not mean you know how to use it to full effectiveness, until you learn how. Even those with strong enough wings still had to learn how to fly, and practice, to become skillful. It was the same with other abilities, including mental strengths, and emotional ones, too. All of the rules were still the same, but also much different, since everyone in the world which was now present was so extremely different than they had been in the old Earth. Then they had to learn to live with other men and women. Here, they had to learn to live with other supermen, and superwomen, too. That alone made things quite different. Also, projects could take centuries, now, and no one seemed to mind, unless it was on a specific schedule as ordered by King Jesus. No one ever wanted to mess up His timing on anything. In this world, everybody loved King Jesus, and wanted to obey and please Him, in all things.

The angels had been carrying large shiploads of many things to the new planets, and the supply convoys had been running around the clock, except for every Sabbath, as timed from Jerusalem. (No matter what part of the solar system where anyone was located, everyone's watches were set to their own time zone, but the calendar was ruled from Jerusalem, and every Saturday was still the Sabbath, just as it had always been, ever since Genesis.) The things which they were taking to the new planets included algae, and mosses, to start producing much more oxygen, and trees had been planted, and the dirt had been enriched, softened, fertilized, watered, and seeded with many different types of plants. The long term goal was to entirely recreate the whole biosphere of Earth, first with the environment, and the climate, and then with the green growing plants, so that in a few hundred years, humans could also live and walk on the two new planets, without the need for a spacesuit. The next phase of the operation was still a century away, when microbes and then insects would be added into the new worlds. There were no more mosquitoes, ticks, fleas, lice, or any other sort of thing that would dare to bite a human, or one of their pets. No creature alive in this age was ever going to be that stupid again. Now, everyone understood that King Jesus would not tolerate anything that tried to hurt one of His Own little brothers or sisters. Every person or thing that had hurt any of them in the last world was either already dead, or was finishing dying, as they paid back King Jesus, for their sins. The payback was only done in the Lake of Fire, but that had all been locked away, somewhere else, so no one had to hear the doomed ones screaming as they died.

An obvious need was more water on each of the new planets, but King Jesus knew just where He had stored up many large comets, of a special type, since they were all composed of over 90% water ice, versus ammonia ice, or anything else. As time had passed, King Jesus had caused many of them to slam into the surfaces of both of the new planets, and the total liquid water on the surface of each world was increasing rapidly. Within 500 years, both worlds would have large oceans, and many, many lakes and rivers, and life would not have to go thirsty, anywhere it walked.

As it had happened once before, seven years earlier, back in Year Six, at high noon, today, Day One, of Year Thirteen, a mighty angel blew a long, loud note from a huge shofar, as he stood upon the porch of the Temple. He proclaimed that in one year, less a day, everyone was required to be within the borders of Israel, by sunset. Another special celebration was being planned by King Jesus, and everyone was ordered to be there to see it all. People spread the word, and everyone began to shut down whatever they had to shut down, to allow enough time for storage and maintenance, and then for travel time to Israel, although that had improved very much in the last few years. New highways were constantly being built, but most effort was going into high speed maglev rail systems, which ran trains at 400 miles an hour and better, on the straight stretches. A lot of people and freight could be moved around that way, and they were, more and more.

As the last day, of Year Thirteen, was ending, and the Sun was settling toward the horizon, all of the people in the world were already within the boundaries of Israel, since they wanted to obey, and they also did not want to miss a moment of whatever spectacular show the good Lord had planned for them tonight. People were still constantly retelling the story of watching Him create two new planets, right before their eyes, even though every one of them, except the children born since that night, had been there in person to witness it all.

As sunset officially began, and light began to fade, the same mighty angel appeared upon the porch of the Temple, and blew a loud, long note upon the giant shofar, and then shouted, "Hosanna!" As he said this, all of the angels of Heaven suddenly appeared in the evening sky around Jerusalem, glowing brightly, and responded, "Baruk Hashim Adoni!" After they said this, they vanished instantly.

The great angel shouted, "Light your candles!" As all the population of the Earth fumbled in the increasing darkness to comply, the angel blew another loud, long note upon the shofar, and vanished as he shouted, "Behold our KING!"

Suddenly, King Jesus appeared over the Temple Mount, just as He had done seven years earlier. He shouted, "Shalom, Havarim! I have another wonderful evening planned for us, to celebrate our second Sabbath Year! Two more planets are enough for us all to work with right now, but I do see a need for a giant, permanent, sustainable space station, since we have many plans for the future, which will be expedited by the use of a base of operations which can support not only factories in space, but also support the human staff, which will work and live there. Some of the things which we will make require low gravity, and some require vacuum, and some require extreme cold. The space factories must be built where they can be stable, accessible, and effective in producing whatever we need from them. Even a factory in space is going to bear good fruit in this

Kingdom, or it will not be part of My Kingdom anyway!"

King Jesus went on, "We already have a place prepared, and ready to use, except that we have a lot of design and installation of all of the factories, and all of the quarters, and all of the power supplies, and all of the transportation, and all of everything else we will want to have online there. You know that the New Year, and the month, always begins with a new moon. Tonight is a new moon, and so it is dark, which actually suits our purposes better, for the sake of easy visibility."

King Jesus said, "Now, blow out your candles, and watch the dark face of the moon with Me!" As the people obeyed, King Jesus caused the moon to appear greatly magnified in everyone's sight, so that it literally filled the sky! The people all felt goose bumps, as they had seven years earlier.

As everyone watched the dark, but still faintly visible moon, the Lord said, "Now, I am going to show you all things that are not yet happening right now, but will start a year from now, after the Sabbath Year is ended. A year is too soon, but if you look up in three more years, with a telescope, you will see the same things you are about to see tonight. Behold!"

As He said this, several green and red lasers lit at many points around the moon, in close orbit, all of them aimed down to the lunar surface at precise locations, and angles. As was the case in the previous demonstration, everything was shown in extreme, high speed, fast forward, time-lapse mode, so the events unfolded quite rapidly before them. As everyone watched, the giant lasers bored holes into the rock crust of the moon. Some were at shallow angles, but some were at very steep angles, and began to bore huge drill holes deeper and deeper into the moon's structure. The rock and dust which was constantly being vaporized by the lasers was being pulled out into the surface, by the ambient vacuum, where the clouds of atomized dust and molten granite molecules flew high above the lunar surface, until the weaker gravity finally slowed them to a stop, thousands of feet in the "air", at which time the dust had all cooled into solid micro-sized rocks again, and came "raining" down on the surface like a hail storm of sand and talcum powder, except that it fell straight down, without any atmosphere to hold it up longer. It left growing piles of dust and rock in a large donut around each bore sight. Any of it which fell back into the stream of the laser was just instantly re-vaporized, and flew back up again along with the fresh material. The lasers cleared their own path through the dust, by flashing it into oblivion upon contact.

Other activity could also be detected, since tiny machines with headlights on them were moving around the surface, each one or group of vehicles racing around to complete its' own missions. Some were very repetitious, and were likely regular supply or transportation lines. At certain locations, for unknown reasons, such as where main vehicle pathways crossed, many new lights began to glow, brighter, and brighter, as more and more buildings and people were moving there and setting up shop, whatever strange business they were about. King Jesus startled all of them, as they stared upward, lost in the spectacle, when He suddenly said, "Yes, some of you will be the people that you are now watching build the cities and factories upon the moon. I will leave you each to wonder, until the time is right, if you will be one of the ones we are watching tonight!"

He went on, after a few more minutes of watching the moon's colonization and taming, as if musing aloud to Himself,

"Yes, the moon was necessary for the particular ecology of Earth, but I had this in mind for it all along."

Then He pointed up at some of the parts of the work, as He said, "That complex of lights that you see down by the lower pole is a great laboratory, and factory, which uses the almost-zero cold, and the vacuum atmosphere, to fabricate some of our most advanced electronics components, for our newest machines and systems. The power supplies all come from the bright side of the moon, whichever direction that may be, depending upon the time of the month, but it includes the entire surface, near the equator, where we have installed huge solar arrays, and we will not have any power shortages there, as long as I keep the Sun shining! The lasers are mounted upon many satellites around the moon, which are also for communications and navigation. The streaking lights which you see moving at a fast rate across the surface are many high speed rail lines, maglev, and they move at about a thousand miles per hour, because of the lighter gravity, and the total lack of air resistance."

He went on, "The bore holes which you are seeing being built at the steepest angles are for mining purposes, since the moon brought a lot of metals and other minerals with it, when I caused it to split off from its' original planet, and wind up here with Earth. The bores done at shallower angles are for great tunnels, within which many more high speed trains will connect all of the parts of the moon, both the near side, and the far side, for rapid transit, and for fast freight moving, too. There will also be carved huge underground caverns, which will have breathable air, light, water, a comfortable temperature, and many green growing things, and these areas will be the main living quarters, and will have observation skylights and ports installed, so people can always look out and see the sky. It will be a special place of study, work, fun, and growth, and there will be a lunar university, where our best students can go and study things there, where they could nowhere else."

He gave all of them a few moments to digest all of this, and then He said, "One of the primary purposes for which I have initiated all of this is that we are going to build many new spaceships. These are going to be about the size of a rather large city, about 20 miles in diameter, and about 140 miles long. They are going to be too heavy to actually land on a planet's surface, but will be long distance, high capacity cargo vessels, to carry people, animals, supplies, and just about everything we can fit into them, along for the ride. Yes, some of you which are listening to this tonight are going to be the ones traveling on those ships, but some of them have not yet been born."

He went on, "These vessels will not at first be interstellar, but only interplanetary, as transports between Shalom, and his brother planets, Ahava, and Lehaim. The large ships will depart from lunar orbit, and then orbit the destination planet, using many large shuttle craft to ferry loads from ship to planet. We will also install Earth-moon ferries, and build a space elevator as close to Jerusalem as possible, which will lift things from the surface to orbit, where they will be taken to lunar orbit, and loaded onto the major ships, or sent down to lunar base by another space elevator there. We are already starting the production of the monofilament molecule chains which will be the unbreakable, but almost weightless wires which make the space elevators possible."

He paused a moment, and then said, "Now, watch this!"

As soon as He said that, a huge green column of fire erupted from the dark surface, not far from the polar factory/laboratory. It was the burn through of a laser from the far side, which could be seen to have been cut at a shallow angle, and it had just completed carving a tunnel for the new trains!

As the crowd smiled, and cheered with joy, King Jesus said, "Okay, now I want to show you one more special thing. Moon, light up, and show us the Sea of Tranquility, please."

Instantly, the moon obediently grew bright, and zoomed in close, to present the Sea of Tranquility, glaring in the sunlight, instead of dark, and all of the people blinked a few times at the dazzle. The scene zoomed in even further, causing gasps of awe and a little thrill of fear in the people. As it settled into stillness, the people could actually see a few little machines, and some tracks in the lunar dust, and the remains of the first L.E.M., and one motionless American flag, still perfectly still and stiff, almost seventy years after it had been planted there. They could even make out micro sized little boot prints in the dust, near wherever the machines and the flag were, and also some moon-buggy tire tracks, and even one of the moon buggies.

As everyone watched, fascinated, the Lord said, "All right, this is the only thing from the old world which has been left completely as it was, in honor of the twelve fearless men which I sent to walk upon this other world. Although you did not know it then, and they themselves did not know, either, each one of them was a direct blood line descendant of one of the twelve tribes of Israel, one from each tribe. The children of Israel are the only ones which ever yet walked upon this new, strange world. Notice that I brought all of them home safe to you again. Now, so the construction processes do not destroy any of this part, watch what our friends the angels are doing right now, live, real time, as we watch from the here, while they work!"

Suddenly, the view zoomed out a little bit, and everyone could see the whole area, where men had ever walked or driven upon the moon. As they all watched, hypnotized, they saw hundreds of mighty angels slowly and carefully lower a gigantic glass dome over the entire zone. The thing was huge, over twenty miles in diameter, and stood over a hundred yards high. No machinery of man could have formed it, or lowered it into place, but the angels set it down without even raising any of the lunar dust while they did it!

The Lord said, "You can take my Word for it that the glass is unbreakable, since it is made out of My Word, and My Promise that this will remain here forever!"

As the people began to wildly cheer and shout "Hosanna!" again and again,

King Jesus said, loudly enough for all of them to hear, "Okay, one more thing!"

The camera view zoomed in, right through the new glass dome, and went close up to a small little notch in the rock ridges behind the scene of the first landing sites, and there rising up out of the flat surface of the dust, almost hidden from notice, in the wild landscape, was a little stone column, which stood about three feet high, all by itself, as if placed there deliberately, although it was a natural formation. Resting solidly, and very comfortably, on top of the little six-inch diameter, three foot-high column, was a little, round, mysterious stone.

King Jesus explained, "This little stone was noticed, and taken back to Earth, which is now named Shalom, by some of the astronauts. They called it the "Genesis Rock". They were right. I set this stone upon this little column as I began your world, in dedication to this forward time, when we will walk upon this little world, as we do upon our own, now. Even though the moon has nowhere near enough gravity to hold an atmosphere, I have other ways I can, and will use, to make a breathable Earth-type atmosphere present upon the moon, and I will teach you how, in the years ahead! Now you see My plan for the moon. Someday, it too will be covered with green plants, air, lakes, and even a small ocean or two. People and animals will wander free over the moon's surface, bounding high in the air, because there will be air there to bound up into! It will be like living in a strange dream, all of the time, but one that is a wonderful delight! It will become the favorite vacation spot of all time, once we are finished with it. It will take about five hundred years to reach that point. We have a lot of hard work ahead to do all of these things. Do you all want to continue on, after this next Sabbath Year, of rest?"

Every one of all the people shouted, "Yes!"

King Jesus went on, "Okay, then, go home, rest, celebrate, but keep these things in the back of your minds, and, when the year is up, come see us in Jerusalem, and sign up on the list, and apply, if you want to go work there! I know all of you can pass the background check, in fact all of you did, or you would not be here!"

As He finished saying this, the moon zapped back to where it was supposed to be, or actually, King Jesus just turned off the zoom lens, and, as the first light of dawn was beginning, He lifted up His arms over them, and said, "Now I bless all of you, and I will see some of you in a year, when we start up again. Discuss all of it with your families, since everyone will be affected by your choices. You will be looking at millions of stars all of the time, so if that does not sound like a job you would like, let someone else volunteer, since I know we will have plenty. Shalom!"

ISRAEL'S LADDER

When the first day of Year 20 arrived, a familiar pattern was repeated, at precisely high noon, in the center of Jerusalem. A mighty angel flew down to the front porch of the Temple, and stood there, and then held up a huge shofar, and sent forth a tremendous blast of announcement. He proclaimed that in a year, minus a day, from right now, everyone on planet Earth was ordered to be present and accounted for, physically, within the borders of old Israel, no later than the sunset.

All of the people present within earshot instantly cheered, as soon as they heard that news. They knew that it meant that King Jesus was planning something magnificent once more, for the kickoff celebration for the next year of Sabbath, which would be Year 21. Everyone immediately went home, to begin preparations for the once-every-seventh-year event!

As the next year passed, people shut down their projects, and closed up their shops, with everyone running full throttle, right up to the last minute. Transportation was vastly improved, with hundreds of new high speed rail lines, crisscrossing the entire land surface of the Earth, as people had needs to gain and maintain access to remote regions, to continue ecological repair work upon the environment, and also, to mine and transport needed raw materials, such as metals and timber. The progress made was truly miraculous, with the atmosphere completely restored, and most of the land regions cleaned up, and most of the remaining effort needed was concentrating upon things like reforestation, and replanting the Great Plains areas with new grass seeds, and wheat, and corn, and many more crops and plants, of which about half of the types were species that had not been alive and well upon the Earth since the days of the Garden of Eden. The other primary projects were still the oceans, and all of the whole world's water supply, which had radically improved. The next phases were the repopulation of those newly restored waters with all of the fish and other water creatures that were needed again, for a living world. Birds were already appearing over greater and greater areas, and some had begun to follow migratory patterns again. The good Lord had once more returned His full blessing upon the world, since He had finished removing evil out of it. Everything grew much faster, and bigger, and better. Projects were completed on time, or ahead of schedule, and always under budget, and always with greater than expected results, and with side-effect fringe benefits, as bonus surprises, cheerfully given by a loving God, which loves to delight His children! Things always worked the way they were supposed to work, but never had, before!

Other worlds were also changing, under the direction and control of King Jesus. Ahava was rapidly becoming a habitable world, as the average temperature had normalized enough so that things like plants could survive, and even begin to thrive and spread there, so, therefore, the good Lord had sent many angels there, carrying a lot of seeds, and had them scatter them every where. The biggest problem with Ahava was still the absence of oceans, but the Lord was working on that aspect, too, by constantly pelting the new planet with large comets, special comets, which He had prepared for this time. The comets were almost entirely water ice, as opposed to ammonia, or some other type of comet ice material. This was because the good Lord had salvaged them from the oceans of Mars. They had been exploded into space, when the star without light, a very tiny singularity, with a radius of only a few meters, had split Mars into two things: Mars, as it was, after the split, and the moon, which was dragged away by the gravity of the singularity, as it headed for, and then smashed into the Earth. This had all happened even before dinosaurs walked upon Earth, but the pieces of the puzzle were already being placed, precisely, accurately, by King Jesus, even then. He used the moon as a counter balance for Earth, and to control the tides, of both of the oceans, the ocean of water, and the ocean of air. The singularity had also captured part of the iron core from Mars, and brought its' extra mass along to the core of the Earth, making Earth the heaviest and densest of the remaining inner planets, with enough mass to hold an atmosphere, and liquid water, and also to be able to generate a huge magnetic field, worldwide, for radiation shielding from solar flares. The impact had nicely knocked away most of Earth's excessive atmosphere, leaving behind a pleasant, and breathable mixture known in modern times as "air". Also, it was now a transparent atmosphere, so that men could look up at the sky, and wonder about God.

The planet formerly known as Mercury, and now named Lehaim, was undergoing radical change, as well. Oceans had also been missing from that world, and it was now also receiving much imported water ice by means of the comet express, and would eventually have oceans, lakes, and rivers upon it as well. Another problem to overcome upon Lehaim was a lack of real topsoil, of which there was abundance upon Earth, and also there was plenty upon Ahava. Some soil was there, upon Lehaim, from the recovered debris after the collision between Mars and Venus, but still, more fertile soil was needed. The original "soil" of Mercury had been a hard-baked crust of "regolith" (a silica, iron, and other minerals confetti mix) which was saturated with helium-3, which would, from now on, forever, be heavily mined and purified and used, in over a thousand different ways, including the final missing piece of the puzzle to reliably produce clean, no-radiation cool nuclear fusion power. (A shoebox full of helium-3 would run whole planet's energy needs for over a year!) Rather than take soil from either of the other two brother worlds, the good Lord was instead causing many asteroids to impact upon Lehaim, which broke up into smaller fragments much more easily, and sometimes even burned away into dust, as they entered Lehaim's brand new atmosphere. It was already about the same precise density and composition of the atmosphere of Earth, as the Lord sped the changes that men and angels were all working so hard to achieve. It was almost as if the good Lord was also eager to complete the major first steps of the restoration and expansion projects, so all men could walk all over the whole solar system, barefooted, without spacesuits!

The projects upon the moon were moving full speed ahead, too. From the surface of the Earth, on a clear night, people could see the giant lasers cutting yet more tunnels and mine shafts deep into the core of the moon. When the night phase of the moon was facing Earth, people could see the sparkling lights of the cities and factories upon the surface, and could faintly trace the spider web of high speed rail lines, as they knit together the whole surface of the moon. All of the old astronauts were working there, at Astronaut City, or back upon Earth, at the new and greatly expanded department of space travel, the J.A.S.A., the Jesus Almighty Space Agency. More efficient rockets were now being used, which used special chemical isotopes for solid fuel, which was atomized in precise amounts, and provided much higher efficiency thrust per pound than the old rockets had ever done. These smaller, modern era rockets could make it to the moon and back, including Earth launches, and moon surface launches, also, over four round trips, before needing more fuel. Running out of gas was never going to be allowed to be a problem, with J.A.S.A. Heat shields were not an extra weight to drag around either, since the Lord had taught men how to make the ships entirely of titanium, and had also shown them how to perfectly reflect light, and heat, by an electronic field applied to the titanium hull, when needed, so that light and heat could not enter the ship at all. The throttle controls upon the vessels were so precise, that they were very comfortable to fly, since you could more gradually increase acceleration, to achieve escape velocity, without being smashed into your chair. It might take a little longer to achieve orbit, but with plenty of fuel, and gentle, but constant acceleration, why almost kill yourself getting into orbit, if you could still get there, a little slower? (It was not quite smooth enough to drink a cup of coffee during liftoff, but maybe, as more refinements were made, it might be, someday.)

So, over the next year, people found stopping places for their projects, and shut down their businesses, and everyone arranged travel back to Israel, once more. People were so excited that they could not stop chattering about what spectacular wonder King Jesus was going to do with them this time! He had convinced them all at the first two celebrations, that He loved doing wonderful things, in a splendid and overwhelming way. There were no secrets in this clean world, but sometimes He did not tell them until the time was just right. Like a parent loves to prepare a wonderful gift for his child, and then, at the right time, to mark a special occasion, present the gift to the child, to forever mark and commemorate the special occasion, and its' significance in the child's life, so the Lord loved to surprise all of His children of this Age with marvels untold, before He revealed them for everyone at once.

As sunset began, every single human being in the whole world was squeezed into the old borders of Israel, as it was in David's time. This time there were teenagers present, also, and some of the older ones had even been to all of the festivals, even if they were just infants at the first one. None of the children of this Age had yet reached 21, because this Age would not itself be 21, until tomorrow morning.

As the sky darkened to a deeper blue, and the first stars began to appear, suddenly, the great angel appeared upon the porch of the Temple, and without any delay, except for the candle-lighting event, the angel blew one great note upon the shofar, and shouted, "Behold our KING!"

The angel vanished instantly, and King Jesus appeared above them, about a mile above the Temple, as He had done upon the previous occasions. As He looked around Him, and saw each and every person there, for a split second, Eye-to-eye, He smiled at them, and said, "Shalom!"

He then stretched out His mighty arms, and His glorious wings, and looked up at the sky, and said, "Now you can see for your selves, that I am indeed the ultimate Man of My Word! I promised you a new Heaven, and a new Earth, and we have already begun. I am glad to have you with Me, to help Me rebuild everything, this time around!"

He went on, "We have a lot to see tonight, so let's get started. Please extinguish your candles, now, and look with Me, not up to the sky this time, but down to the due south of here, down at horizon level. Okay, General Armstrong, are your astronauts ready?"

Suddenly the entire crowd could clearly hear the voice of General Neil Armstrong, as he answered, "Yes, Sir!"

The Lord spoke again, and said, "All right, then, on My countdown: 10, 9, 8, 7, 6, 5, 4, 3, 2, 1, 0, Ignition!"

As He finished, two bright spots instantly appeared, low down, just below the horizon, but very bright, like a small twin sunrise. One was due south, and the other was a bit more to the right, or south by southwest. As they continued to watch, the brightness increased rapidly, until two new tiny suns burst above the horizon line and then streaked upward into the night sky, flooding the whole landscape with brief light, like two flare pistols, and then continuing to accelerate upwards into space.

While they were watching, King Jesus was telling them, "You have seen how we have already laid the foundation for expansion, with the creation and terra forming of the new planets, and the settling and development upon the moon. These are two of the new solid fuel rockets, with titanium hulls, which will serve as our planet jumpers, since they are designed to enter and leave a planet's atmosphere and gravity well without difficulty. They can climb into orbit quite slowly, but the fine astronauts aboard those ships tonight said it would be okay with them to show you a very high speed launch, for demonstration purposes. Even so, the acceleration was increased by geometric progression, doubling every 30 seconds, so that the full crush of the acceleration never hits them all at once. Now, why are we launching them tonight? Watch!"

As He said this, two small bright dots suddenly appeared in the sky, right in front of where the ships were still moving, but with much reduced flames. The two ships flipped over, as though performing a rehearsed move, and instantly flared their rockets even brighter than they had when achieving orbit.

Jesus said, "What you see are the two forgotten moons of Mars: Phobos, and Deimos. I have moved them here to their new assigned positions, and the ships are about to land upon them. Notice that the rockets are flaring much brighter now, as the pilots are using double the thrust which they employed during launch. This is so they can shorten the travel and landing time, or we could not show you all of this in a single night, at least not in real time, like this is tonight. This part is exciting, but there is more to follow."

As He finished for a moment, suddenly the zoom lens effect was applied, and everyone saw clearly the two small moons, and watched the ships land flawlessly upon each of them. A few minutes later, hatches opened on the hulls of the ships, and large all-terrain forklift things carried out huge spools of some strange, sparkling, iridescent material. Each ship only unloaded one enormous spool, but it was larger than a house. The forklifts placed them at particular locations, and the ship's crews began to use lasers to drill quick, deep holes into the solid rock of the small moons surfaces. Then they installed anchor bolts, specially made of a type of metal, which no one had even known existed, before King Jesus showed them where to find it, and how to process it. It was, when prepared correctly, able to be melted and poured like wax into molds, and, if mixed with another previously unknown mineral, acted like a stainless steel version of epoxy, and became unbreakable, short of nuclear destruction. After they had corkscrewed the anchors deep into the bedrock, they began to un-spool the sparkly tape, as it appeared to be. They took the loose end and carried it back to the ship, where they attached it to the very nose of the vessel, by means of a special hook. About halfway down the hull of the ships, special arms were activated, and came straight out, with a lockable ring to secure the tape when launching, to hold it out of the flame of the rocket. An additional weight was attached to the tape, about a hundred yards further down. The crews checked the mountings for the two spools, and climbed back aboard the ships. As if fired by the same trigger, the two ships leaped into the sky again, each one trailing the sparkly tape behind them.

As they launched, King Jesus said, "Okay, phase one is complete. Now we have new planets, a new space station, new space ships, and new visions of what we are going to do with our greatly expanded real estate. We still are missing an essential piece of the puzzle, however. We need a way to take the problems out of the leg of the journey which goes from the surface to orbit. Until now, that either had to be done by rocket, or angel. Now, we are going to start doing it a different way. The reason that the "tape" you see is sparkly is that it is saturated with nano-diamonds. These are only formed as a result of cataclysmic events, but, between the destruction done by Ceres when it vaporized a lot of the Pacific Ocean, and the formation of the new planets, finding an abundant supply of nano-diamonds is not a problem for our friends the angels, and we gathered them into our factories upon the moon, and used those nano-diamonds as a type of condensation nuclei for the formation of carbon nano-fiber monofilament strands, over a mile in length, and thousands of times greater in strength, than anything which was produced in the old world. Using these super-threads, we were able to finally produce a cable long enough and strong enough to serve well in the design and construction of the first space elevator in the universe!"

As He paused, the zoom view zapped back to normal, and people could see the two dots that were the little moons, and the little flying torches that were the two ships. The ships were pointed straight down, right back toward the places where they had launched. King Jesus went on, "Now, notice that the ships will soon flip over, and point their torches toward the ground again, to slow their descent. The pilots will take care not to burn the cable with their torches, although it likely would not hurt it, if it did not go on for too long. The cable is okay for up to several thousand degrees, since it was made in temperatures hotter than that. It is also impervious to radiation, short of nuclear detonation, and impact will not hurt it, either, unless something like a spaceship with a titanium hull flew into it at high speed. You might think that the nano-diamonds would add too much weight, and therefore make the cable impractical, but that is not the case, since they are about the size of a molecule, and are much more sparsely scattered throughout the strands than you might guess. They act as anchor points, to which the strands attach. They are the connectors between the fibers, which function makes the ultra long strands a possibility, and also adds some measure of material toughness, since, after all, they are still as tough as any other diamond. Now, watch the pilots make their drops!"

As He paused, the two ships came to a virtual hover, a mile or so above the ground (which everyone could watch, because King Jesus had activated the zoom lens effect again) and released the ends of the cables, which promptly fell to the ground, with red flashing beacons on the drop weights. The two ships then increased their flames, and moved away into the night, to go land somewhere else. As they cleared the area, two helicopters arrived, and landed, one for each cable end, and they unloaded a jeep from each of the large helicopters, and drove off into the night with the ends of the cables. The helicopters lifted off, and escorted the jeeps along in the darkness.

King Jesus spoke again, "The reason why we launched from where we did tonight is so you could see where the anchor points for the cables will be, here on Earth. The ends will be anchored deep underground, and made very secure, indeed. The far ends will be further secured, before we use the cables to lift anything at all. The cable may be nearly unbreakable, and it is, but we still have to hold down the weight of two small mountains of rock, even if Phobos is only 13.8 miles in diameter, and Deimos is only 7.8 miles in diameter. They will be finally positioned at the heights of 62,000 miles, and 65,000 miles, with Phobos being the higher anchor. Deimos will be the first, or most eastward, anchor, located at the equator, five miles inland from a town named Kismaayo, Somalia. Space elevators must be anchored upon the equator, or they will not work. The closest point at a shoreline, upon the equator, due south of Jerusalem, is Kismaayo, Somalia. We need to place it near a shore line, since much of our freight for it, and from it, will move by sea. The second cable will be anchored 1200 miles to the west, five miles inland from Libreville, Gabon. This is the next closest point on a shoreline, due south, or almost due south, of Israel. Phobos will be anchored there, and tied at a higher altitude, by three thousand miles. If the impossible ever did happen, and something or somebody fell off of the first anchor, then Phobos would be able to scoop them up, before they were lost in space. If they fall off of Phobos, I will have to send an angel to catch them. The anchors will be fixed in another few minutes, and we will leave them both alone, after we quickly tension the cables to the altitude we want. We will rest the crews and the project, for this Sabbath Year, and then resume, a year from now. If the cables stay unbroken, and solidly attached, for this next year, we know they will keep lasting, since we will even more securely anchor the ends, all around, before we use them. Okay, General Armstrong, are you and General Aldrin and your crews finished anchoring and tensioning the cables, or do you need a little longer?"

Immediately, everyone heard the general answer back, "We're all done, Sir! Mission accomplished!"

A large smile flashed across the face of King Jesus, and everyone else cheered, when they heard "mission accomplished". Jesus said, "Well done, gentlemen! Knock off, and have a great year's well-earned rest!"

Then He looked down at everyone there below Him, and said, "Now, as the Sun begins to rise, I bless you all, and wish you a grand year of rest, and wanted for you to see one last thing before we go. Look!"

He pointed south again, and the Sun was just beginning to light the newly installed sparkly cable, and, as the Sun rose rapidly over the eastern horizon, the cables were illuminated with dazzling fire, starting at the top, and racing down toward the Earth! It looked like two slow-motion fiery laser beams were speeding down from the small moons, slowed down enough to see them travel, as through molasses. Even though the cables actually diverged, since each one extended out in a straight line, from the center of the Earth, through its' anchor point, the lines appeared perfectly parallel, when seen from Earth, because of perspective, as when looking down a railroad track. The two visual effects precisely offset each other, and the thing looked like two giant strings of light, like the rails of a huge ladder, reaching all the way into Heaven. As everyone watched, hundreds of thousands of angels flew up and down the cables, all along their entire lengths, inspecting, to be sure no damage had occurred during the installation process.

Suddenly, King Jesus appeared between the cables, standing upon the Earth, but stretching so tall that His Head was at the same altitude as the small moons! He laughed a hearty laugh, which shook the whole planet a little bit, as if the great Earth was also laughing with Him, and said, "All right, now you see what the big surprise was for this Sabbath Year. The only way I could keep it secret was to do it all on the far side of the moon! Man, you guys are curious, all the time! Now, go home, rest, and get back to work a year from now, because we are just getting started. Travel well, and rejoice along the Way, and shalom!" As He said this, He vanished.

Two of His first apostles had been standing by the porch of the Temple, watching the whole thing, as He revealed it through the night. Philip noticed the strange look upon the face of his friend, Nathanael, and asked him, "What are you thinking?"

Nathanael cleared his throat, and focused upon Philip, as if returning from a far distance, in his mind, and said, "He just showed it to me!"

Philip looked puzzled, and asked, "What?"

Nathanael smiled at the memory, and then explained, "The day that I met King Jesus, do you remember what He told me? He said that I would one day see Heaven opened, and the angels of God, ascending and descending, upon the Son of Man!"

As they both paused a moment, to think about how vast His knowledge was, and how amazingly detailed, even thousands of years in advance, they both heard His voice, as He chuckled softly in their minds, and clearly said to them, "I told you that I was a Man of My Word!"

NEW MOON

There was a fresh, new smell and feel to the cool spring breeze this day, as if even the whole planet eagerly awaited the upcoming spectacular ceremonies. By this time, even the fabric of Creation itself began to hold its' breath, whenever the Year of Sabbath was approaching. Every celebration brought universe-changing wonders, and every person alive always got to watch them happen, right before their own eyes!

This would be the fourth such occasion, since the return of King Jesus Christ. Today was the first day of Year 27, and next year would be a seventh year, a year of Sabbath, and rest. As before, at high noon, a great angel flew down to the porch of the Temple, sounded a great shofar, and then decreed that everyone must be present and accounted for, in precisely one year, minus one day, no later than sundown, the last day of year 27. People excitedly went rushing about their close-up-year business, as they prepared to travel to Israel, and to be there on time, for the festival.

Things had continued to progress well since the last Sabbath Year, and it seemed like taking one year out of every seven off, to rest, and give thanks, had proven to be the missing piece of the puzzle as to the age-old mystery concerning how to best live a productive, effective, and satisfied life. People returned from their Sabbath Years with refreshed hearts, and clear, bright minds, and strengthened, re-energized bodies. Sometimes, during the time off, brilliant new ideas and inventions came to them, in vivid dreams, and visions, often straight from King Jesus, in Person. (These events happened whenever it suited the King, whether the person was asleep, or not.)

The space elevators were both up and running very routinely, without ever having had any accident, or failure. In the old days, people had made things okay, but not well enough to last a thousand years at a time, without maintenance. These days, men and angels worked together, as co-workers at the Royal factories of King Jesus Christ, both upon the Earth, and now, also upon the moon! The lunar factories were going full blast, and many new projects were accelerating exponentially, requiring almost continual launches from both the Earth and the moon, of the now 50 ships which used the new solid fuel isotope rockets. The ships passed each other constantly, as they raced across the gap between the Earth and the moon, carrying people and equipment. Almost all of the raw materials which were required upon the moon for the new industrial factories were locally available, since the gigantic mining tunnels had been in full swing now for years. A steady flow of load after load of rocks was processed around the clock, all cut and blasted out of the deep, dark inner treasure stores within the moon. No, the moon was not as dense as the Earth, but it still had plenty of minerals hidden inside, including very much gold, silver, iron, and even a surprising amount of uranium. More surprising still, it had a lot of water, stored in polar craters, and under rocks, deep below, as ice. That showed very good foresight on the part of the Creator, since, where people live, they must have a lot of water.

The people usually traveled by rocket, which could achieve orbit much quicker, but the loads of heavy specialized equipment were always sent up into orbit by space elevator. In the old world engineers had thought to make the runners, or lifters, of the space elevators move upward at a speed of about 200 miles an hour. That sounds pretty good, but these, the real, working ones, in the real world-to-come, streaked up and down the cables at over a thousand miles an hour, no matter how much weight they were lifting. They could actually move at twice that speed, but the human operators usually liked it better at around a thousand. The space elevators were transparent, and the view was always stunning. Lots of tourists came just to ride them up and back down, one time, for the fun of it. The things were huge, with a lifting bay of 100 yards square, which was entirely pressurized. The hull had the same auto-opaque properties as did the spaceships' hulls. No one wanted to fight the full glare of raw sunlight beyond the atmosphere. The power capacity for the lifters was almost limitless, since they had direct drive motors, with magnetic suspension bearings, and these huge motors were energized by gigantic ground based L.E.D. lasers, which were sparked by nuclear reactors. Each space elevator had a dozen reactors online to power it around the clock. The enormous lasers were the same design as the emitters used upon the moon, but lower in intensity, by an order of magnitude or two, so they did not vaporize the space elevators. (Also, the ones used upon the moon are driven by the new plasma reactors, which can be used safely only in orbit, not upon the surface.)

The space elevator was the more scenic way to go, and the gentler, as far as crushing acceleration might be concerned, but it took longer. To go from Earth to either one of the sky stations took about 72 hours, including loading and unloading time. Each space elevator made one round trip per week, and the whole crew rested the seventh day, as ordered. Every Sunday morning, at sunrise, after the Sabbath had just ended, the crew lit up the lifters, and loaded on board all of the people, and all of the freight that was supposed to go on this trip, and off they went! They always started slow, to give the first-timers a chance to adjust, and then the pilot hit the throttle more and more, until they were zipping upward at over a thousand. The cable always stayed perfectly taught, and the lifters tracked flawlessly straight. There were many places provided for people to lounge, and take naps, and even sleep over night, and they had installed excellent snack bars and restaurants, as well. (In this world, as it was now, it was being run, in all things, by King Jesus Christ, and those who love Him, and even entertainment and education had been provided, too.) There were video presentations, and even some live speakers, to help people understand all of the wonderful science and engineering used in the design and operation of the space elevator system, and all of its' component parts. This time, things were being done right!

The entire chassis of the lifters had been built right in place around the already installed, and tensioned, cable. The balance of the whole mass was critical, so, of course, the cable had to pass through the very center of the lifter. Also, the cable was unbreakable, all made in one unending piece. Consequently, every time one built a space elevator, one had to then build the runner in place around the cable. Anyway, they got it done. (The things were far too massive and huge, to move around on land after they were built.) The anchor points for the cables had to be fully completed at first, anyway, before the runner assembly, at that same location.

Once the lifter had been finished, it had been hoisted up the cable into the air to a height of 200 yards by its' own motors, which had been temporarily hot-wired to power cables from the reactors' output lines. Since it was impractical to try to make a power cord 65,000 miles long, the lasers had to take over, there. Once everyone but the test pilot crew had been cleared of the area, the mammoth L.E.D. lasers directly under the lifter house had been lit, and the solar cells all over the under side of the housing crackled to life with high voltage electricity, like a half-tamed lightning bolt, wanting to break loose from its' bottle! The gigantic enclosed platform, looking like a huge glass tear drop, with many levels and decks visible inside, sprang to life with dozens of brilliant lights all over it, inside, and out! (Some were floods, some were spots, some were just for hallways, and some were nightlights for the children on board, but there were thousands of lights, of all colors.) The monstrous motors began to hum at a low, subsonic rumble, as when one hears the engine of a freight train by bone conduction, through the legs and feet, but not the ears. As people had cheered, the huge assembly had smoothly accelerated upward, racing up the cable, and had vanished slowly into the distance in the sky, as it accelerated to top rated speed, and continued upward, until it had reached all the way to Phobos, where it braked smoothly, to a perfect stop. The return test journey was just as history-making, and smoothly uneventful, as had been the ascent. The elevators had been put into use the next week, and had never stopped, since, except on Saturday, at sunrise, until Sunday morning.

As sunset began, everyone was already within the boundaries of ancient Israel, and the ceremony started and proceeded much as it had on previous occasions for the Sabbath Year celebrations. When the moment came, King Jesus appeared in the air above the Temple, as He had each time before, and said, "Shalom!"

He then went on to briefly summarize the progress that had been gained during the previous years, and then told them

that this would be another close-up look
at the moon. As He said this, the view of
the night sky zoomed in close to the
moon, and people could make out strange
new details and lights, all over the entire
surface. The view continued to zoom
closer and closer, and even passed into
and through the rocks, as King Jesus took
everyone on a visual tour of the new,
enormous, subterranean caverns, carved
deep below the moon's surface, by the
huge industrial mining lasers, and some
parts had even required the invention of
new fiber-optic cable materials, which
had been used to channel the laser beams
around corners, and along all manner of
curved and complex beauties of design
and wonder, which would make the
experience of living within these
chambers a great joy of exploration and
development. The concept of design was
very similar to that which the good Lord
had employed before, at Petra, where
more than a million people could live in

thousands of natural caves, and find shelter, from storm, and war, and heat, and cold. Catacombs had been used many times before in human history, as dwellings, and hiding places. The difference, this time, was profound, however, as these caverns were official government apartments, parks, hotels, shopping malls, theatres, and schools and hospitals, too. People did not come here to hide, but to live, and work, and play, and raise children, and send them to school, too. (People even had pets here, too. Dogs did okay, once they adapted to the lower gravity, but cats always stayed sort of spooked about not being precisely sure about just how high they might fly, whenever they tried to jump up on the bookcase! A few times of bouncing off of the living room ceiling made cats even more nervous than they already were.)

The good Lord showed everyone the matching residential caverns in the equatorial regions, also, as well as the complex web of high speed rail lines that tied the entire surface of the moon all together, just as the Earth had been completely laced with rail lines of its' own. King Jesus also showed them, in high speed, time lapse mode, the newly invented ore-smelting process, that could only work upon the moon, or some other similar place.

The King zoomed in to a huge clear special plastic dome, much taller, but not as vast, as the one protecting the Footprint Museum. At the precise center of the great dome, there was an area of black obsidian, about 100 yards on a side, forming a rough square. It was perfectly flat, as though it had been precisely machined, but the Lord did not bother to explain just how He had done that. Monstrous doors, in the side of the dome, opened, and in rumbled a non stop stream of rail cars full of raw ore, from deep within the moon. Every car looped on the track around the square of obsidian, and ejected its' ore load off the side, as it moved on past. In between the trains, which each had about a hundred cars full of ore, large electric bulldozers pushed the ore into the center of the square rock, and this operation continued, around the clock, for about two whole days and nights, until the whole square area was full of raw ore, stacked four stories high. Then, the equipment and men all left the dome, and it was sealed, tight. Then, all at once, dozens of lasers fired into the dome, hitting the raw ore piled upon the obsidian rock, which acted like a huge plate of high temperature glass, and stayed solid as a rock, even though everything else standing upon it was flash-vaporized! The whole dome filled instantly with hot vaporized rocks and dust, every particle shredded away from its' fellows, and alone, stripped down to become a single atom. The dome had been flooded with nitrogen, which is inert, and would not combine or interact

with the atoms of ore, and also, is
transparent, and so would not be affected
by the laser beams. After a few seconds,
all of the giant lasers, some upon the
lunar surface, and some positioned
above, in orbit, where the largest ones
must always operate, simultaneously shut
off at once, and the dome was filled with
an opaque, hot dust cloud, which at first,
glowed orange, but almost instantly
began to cool to a dull red glow, and then
just to dark gray dust, and it finally began
to start to clear. In real time, the whole
condensation process took about two
weeks, as the heavier elements condensed
first, and fell to ground first, forming a
bottom sedimentary layer, of whatever
was the heaviest element, or bunch of
elements, which the ore load had
contained. The gasses, lightest at top,
would be collected first, and then the
dome would be slowly vented to vacuum,
and the electric bulldozers would come in
again, as well as front end loaders, and

the operators would just scrape up a layer of whatever particular elements were on the list, until all were collected, and neatly sorted out, almost 100% pure, in each case. It was an easy matter to do a secondary refining process, in cases where the purity was of absolute importance, such as with certain metals, and other high value chemicals, such as hydrogen, and oxygen, which made steady water production a thing which could be achieved, and it was already part of the routine. Gold and silver were really becoming commonplace, which was not a mystery, since thousands of tons of raw ore were processed every month. The whole process could not be used upon Earth, however, since vacuum, and the absolute cold of space were necessary conditions to conduct the operation. Also, the low gravity helped to add time for the dust to condense, before it hit the ground. Some exotic metals and ores were found and brought to the moon by some of the solid fuel rockets, which were able to make runs out to the nearer asteroids, just beyond the old orbit of Mars. The Lord showed the pilots which asteroids that He wanted, and they usually looked quite ordinary, but later were found to contain large amounts of one particular metal or mineral or another, and always one that was rare upon the moon. The good Lord knew all the names of every star, and every other creature, so He also knew which asteroid was solid bauxite, for aluminum, or solid iron, for steel, or solid gold, for wiring, or plating, or whatever He wanted.

After He had showed them the polar water factories, where the buried polar ice was being mined and purified, and shipped around the moon, wherever people were, He directed their attention to a particular spot on the equator of the moon, on the day phase side, and had them all watch, as General Neil Armstrong had his astronauts launch another rocket from the base point, and land upon a small, oddly shaped asteroid, named Totutus, which is a little less than three miles long, and only a half a mile wide, at its' narrowest point, where the handle part of a dumbbell would be. In fact, it is shaped about like a dumbbell, or dog bone. The Lord had moved the asteroid into perfect position right over the anchor point, to make it an easy shot to hook up for the astronauts.

As the good Lord continued to narrate and explain all the wonderful things which were being revealed this night, the people watched the astronauts complete the installation of the space elevator cable for the moon. Once they had anchored the spool upon Totutus, they launched from there, and swooped down to the lunar surface, right at the anchor point, and dropped the cable end, with a weight, and a flashing red beacon on it. Another vehicle approached, and two astronauts got out of it, and hooked the end of the cable to their moon-cat, and jumped back into it, and sped off to the final anchor point, to establish the first lunar space elevator, and the first space elevator on another planet, beside Earth.

As these things played out for everyone, the good Lord explained to them that the center part of Totutus was almost entirely composed of titanium, which was one reason why it had retained it's unusual shape. It was a special fragment of the original Mercury, before the Sun lit up, and blew away most of original Mercury into fragments and asteroids. The Lord had reserved Totutus precisely for this purpose. It was the perfect mass to work as the counter weight for the lunar space elevator, being about 1/6th the mass of Phobos. Phobos was spinning around the Earth, always over the same precise point, as was Deimos, and they both were anchored to points moving on the surface of the Earth at 1,000 miles per hour. Totutus was anchored to a point at the equator of the moon, moving at a rate of about 10 miles per hour. Phobos was at a height of 65,000 miles. Totutus was at a height of 11,000 miles. The same precise principles were at work, but the scale of masses and velocities was, in each case, different, so adjustments had to be made. As it turned out, the good Lord once again proved that His math was flawless, and it worked like a charm. He even explained that the titanium extracted from Totutus would be used right there in orbit, to achieve the creation of the mammoth hulls of the huge Ark ships, which would one day carry life to other worlds, which were still under construction. (The scrap rock from the lunar mining operation would be lifted up to Totutus, and used in construction of factories and living quarters there, and a space port. The amount of rock sent there would equal the titanium extracted from

Totutus, so the counterweight would always weigh the same.)

As the people watching saw the cable of the lunar space elevator go taught, a great cheer went up from everyone watching, and that was everyone in the world! People knew what this step meant. Now, it would be a normal, routine part of everyday life, for people to take something, or someone, from upon the surface of the Earth, and three days later, have that person, persons, or equipment arrive smoothly upon Phobos, or Deimos, where a shuttle rocket could load it, and two days later, have that person at Totutus, and a half a day later, land upon the moon, safely, smoothly, and affordably. Average total travel time, one way, Earth to moon, six days. That time frame applied to almost anything, or any number of people, since there were now plenty of shuttle rockets to shuttle the moon run for large groups, and the space elevators could each handle extremely large weights, and big groups of people, too.

King Jesus waited until the roar died down a bit, and then said, "I wanted to show you this final piece of the puzzle tonight, so that all of you know what the main overview of the entire project is all about. Our great grand children will walk upon other worlds, with us, one day! You know that our work on the great ships will soon begin in earnest, now that the materials and platforms are set in place. Those of you wishing to volunteer for moon or other space duty, please contact the placement office in the government building, downtown Jerusalem, on the ground floor. I need systems designers, architects, metallurgists, heavy equipment operators, welders, and pilots. Your background checks are already complete. You all passed! Just come in and tell us what you want to do, and, if your aptitude set works with your request, off you go! Otherwise, we will find you something else, which you will also like. Check first with your families, if you plan to be off planet for an extended time."

"Now, you have seen the mighty things begin, and more will follow. For now, we need to focus upon working still more on the recovery and repopulation of all the different animals and plants which were lost. Even though the space effort is grand and spectacular, we also have to keep up our work on the ground. We are approaching halfway back to recovery for the plants, and about a third of the way back for the animals. We still have more to do."

He paused a moment in thought, and said, "In the Name of the Father, the Savior, and the Holy Spirit, I bless each of you! Go in peace, work in joy, and rest content. You have each done well. Keep on doing so. Progress will continue, and I will also bless and accelerate it, where it does not too much disturb the needed balance in things. Remember, these mighty things we are doing together are dreams coming true for us all, and, we are doing them for the love of our children and grandchildren, and more after them. We want them to also see and know the wonders of the goodness and power of Almighty God!"

He took a deep breath, smiled, and then stretched out His arms over them all, and said, "Until next time: Shalom!"

BOTTLE ROCKETS

It was almost sundown, the last day of Year 34, and tonight would be the official celebration for the Year of Rest, Year 35. It was the fifth time this event had been held. The entire population of the world was all present and accounted for, since attendance was absolutely mandatory.

As had occurred each time before, mighty angels announced the Celebration, and then, they began the opening ceremonies. At the precise moment, when the sky had grown fully into night, King Jesus appeared over the Temple, high enough up so that the people all over the nation of Israel could see Him directly. After the first dazzling flare, He dimmed the glow of His infinite glory, low enough so that everyone could still see Him, but also could see all the night sky behind Him, as He spoke.

"Shalom!" As He said this, His great smile broke out all over everyone, and stirred their hearts immediately, with joy, love, and excitement! They knew from all of the previous festivals that something wonderful and overwhelmingly grand was scheduled to be revealed this night, since the good Lord had already conditioned all of them to expect many strange and wonderful miracles from now on, especially at festival time.

He spent the first few minutes welcoming everyone, and told them that all the amazing projects were right on course, and that many were well ahead of schedule. He explained that His new technology science had taught men how to build and do things of which no one except Him had ever dreamed. He also explained to them how the precise principle of "a day with the Lord is as a thousand years" had been applied to the terra forming changes being wrought upon both Ahava and Lehaim, but which were not being used upon the moon, since the changes in the lunar environment were more technical and scientific, and also industrial, rather than ecological, as the moon was not intended at the present time for open inhabitation, without space suits. Part of what made the moon ideal as the spaceship factory, which was its' primary purpose, was the lower gravity, and even more so, the vacuum, and the near-absolute-zero cold of the south polar region's craters, where special processes could be done, such as growing crystals from metals, which could not normally be achieved in atmosphere, or sometimes in gravity, or sometimes in anything much warmer than 4 degrees Kelvin. The moon might be terra formed someday, but, for now, it had to stay as it was, to be able to do what it was required to do.

The planned ships would be larger than a big city, and some of the largest would be around a hundred miles long. There was no possible way, short of miraculous, to build a ship that large and heavy, if the factory happened to be located upon a large planet, especially if anyone expected the monster sized ship to launch into orbit, especially if the ship was supposed to survive the launch forces, even though the good Lord was teaching men how to build rocket engines easily powerful enough to lift such a behemoth into orbit. The only problem with using those engines inside the Earth's atmosphere would be that the release of a large, hot plume of blue fire over 10 miles long, producing a temperature of about 11,000,000 degrees (about a million degrees hotter than the Sun) might cause some unfortunate results, such as hot gas clouds, from the exhaust plasma, which would disrupt weather patterns all over the earth, perhaps for decades, and could easily produce deadly storms, even if the atmospheric shock waves from the launch plume could be survived. If a nuclear weapon produces shock waves like battleship steel, moving outward at the speed of sound, how much worse would the shock waves from a plasma ignition become?

The concept for the first generation of the new super rockets was based upon an idea that had even been known and developed during the old days, before the King had returned to rule the Universe, openly, and wisely. A scientist named Franklin Chang-Diaz, just outside of Houston, Texas, had invented and developed the first VASIMR rockets, which were the essential design to be used in the first models of the new engines. They operated upon the concept of using high intensity radio waves, like a giant microwave oven, to super heat argon molecules. These argon molecules were thus converted to plasma, achieving temperatures of between a million, and 100 million degrees. The entire hot plasma plume was contained and directed out of the exhaust end of the rocket engine, using intense magnetic fields, which are quite adept at containing and directing super hot plasma, although no solid physical material can possibly contain plasma, since it is even hotter than the Sun. (By the way, VASIMR stands for Variable Specific Impulse Magnetoresponse Rocket.) Later ships would use actual fusion rockets, since that is an effective energy source for high-order propulsion, but the technical problems involved would cause it to be many centuries, even these miraculous days, before mankind could safely develop and harness fusion power as an on-board rocket. Imagine riding around on the front of an exploding nuclear bomb, hydrogen, at that, and see what problems one might encounter.

The reason why a VASIMR engine was better was that it was "variable", so that the plasma was produced in controllable levels. It is extraordinarily difficult to try to throttle down a fusion explosion, like trying to take a rope and lasso a 300 mile-per-hour high speed train. Anyone trying to hold on to the rope would either lose an arm, or be taken for a sudden 300 mile-per-hour ride. Making a hydrogen bomb explode was fairly simple, once you understood enough to use a fission bomb as the blasting cap. Making a fusion reaction smolder along slowly, instead of acting like a flash bulb, was going to take a lot of industrial high-tech science to ever actually achieve, and it would never be possible at all, except that King Jesus had already started teaching the scientists the right way to approach the problem, and it was a surprise to learn from the King that the way to solve the mystery was to learn how to regulate one of the four primary forces. It was not the strong nuclear force, or the weak nuclear force, or gravity. Instead, it was the electromagnetic force inside the hydrogen atom that could be regulated, and intensified, or diffused, as required, to produce a steady, slow flow, instead of an erupting volcano. The next few centuries would give men the needed experience and training in using special magnetic and electrical fields, and applying them precisely, even down to the sub-atomic level. Without that expertise, no sane person would dare to try to build a fusion rocket. Even if they did, they would not volunteer for the test flight!

So, for the present, VASIMR engines would serve very well. They were vastly simpler than old-style rocket motors to build, operate safely, maintain, and repair. They still could produce plenty of thrust, enough to run ships all over the inner planets, and the asteroid belt, but later centuries would be the time for exploring and perhaps settling some of the outer planets, or at any rate, some of their almost Earth-sized moons, like

Titan, or maybe Ganymede. Humans did not yet have all of the necessary technology, or specialized industry, until they could make large fusion rockets, and put them on large ships, since a journey to the outer planets was a matter of years, even with hydrogen rockets pushing the ship.

The design and material for the inner system ships was already a matter of history, and teams were already working on the strong titanium frames for the inner skeletons of the great cargo vessels, and the same type of clear high tech plastic hulls would be used, as were already in use for the solid fuel ships. The same precise material was used in the construction of the domes upon the moon, and also the domes now installed upon all of the space elevator anchor rocks. It was getting to where you could walk a long way under some of the huge, inter-connected domes, and never need to put on a space suit. Some of the "moon people" (which is what they called those living and working there) had formed jogging clubs, which actually amounted more to leaping from one foot to the other, in 20-foot long steps. Some were developing lunar off-road bicycles, which had to be light, and very strong, and have shock absorbers better than those on an Earth bicycle. (When you bounced over a small rise, or hit a rock, in gravity only a sixth as strong as that of the Earth, you were going to do a little air time, and you wanted a great suspension, with a lot of shock-absorbing ability, whenever you slammed back down.)

As had been promised by the good Lord, these days nobody died. It was impossible for anyone to sin, and it was impossible for anyone to die. Even though people could walk out across the lunar surface, unprotected, and not die, or be seriously hurt, it still felt uncomfortable, and no one usually saw any reason to want to do something like that. Emergencies just did not happen any longer, since everyone did the right thing, all the time. There were no wrecks, or any other sorts of disasters. Machines were perfectly built, and did their jobs well. People got along, and actually helped and cared for each other.

One of the other aspects of space flight had always been the limits of the human space suit. At a minimum, we need at least a third of an atmosphere to survive: any less, we die. At least, it was that way in the old days. Now, people could walk outside in vacuum, and freezing, absolute cold, and stay there an hour, or a day, and walk back into the dome, and shake off the chill, and take a deep breath, and rub their cold hands together to warm them, and then go on about their business. Radiation was no problem, either, at least, not for the older adults. As the resurrected children of light grew and matured in their new lives, the strengths and abilities of King Jesus grew ever stronger and more active in each human, individually, as appropriate for that person. As with a child, the strength, wisdom, and supernatural powers grew, as the person grew in the Lord. The more mature in Him, the greater the likeness in abilities between the believer and King Jesus. The cherubs and angels already had all of the power and strength they would ever need, but it was also all they would ever have. The children of light kept on growing stronger and wiser, with every passing year. That would continue with all of them, forever.

So, even though some of the more mature humans did not actually need space suits any longer, at least not for short periods of time, the children and others which had not grown up enough yet in our good Lord still had to wear protection to go outside into vacuum. Even the weakest baby could not die, but space exposure, or radiation, could make them feel terrible, and weaken them drastically, and keep them bed-ridden for a long time, until they could recover. The only reasonable solution for all of that was to invent and perfect effective spacesuits.

The new type of space suit was a far shot from the old type suits. Those things had been essentially inflated balloons, so that enough air pressure could be kept inside, but that caused the suits to be very awkward and unbending. Trying to move around in one of them was like trying to move with a splint on every one of your moving joints, like knees, elbows, and so on. A person could sort of move, but not much, and not easily.

By contrast, the new suits fit like a second skin, and the required pressure was maintained by a system of cords and elastic bands, precisely arranged all over the whole body, wrapping every vulnerable point in a tight, but very flexible shield. The helmets were clear bubbles, but made of the same material as the space ship hulls, and they also had the same selective polarization technology, to shield the person from too much sunlight. The suits themselves were high tech reflective, and could even prevent penetration by x-rays, and even gamma rays. Future developments would produce suits which could shield against even cosmic rays, which are the toughest, and most destructive of all. Even this first generation of suits enabled space folks to move around very easily, and stay outside for days on end, if the project required such a thing.

With all of the fast-paced inventions and constructions occurring these days, it was almost impossible for the ordinary person to keep up with all of the advances and changes. That was one of the reasons why the Lord chose this festival, every seventh year, to update everyone, and let them also see everything which was progressing, since King Jesus did not believe in keeping any secrets from His people. Even though the work would continue and make steady gains, whether anyone else but the King knew about it, or not, it was His wish and joy to share all of the wonders with everybody, as things were being done, and to engineer things so that men and angels could participate in the rebuilding and expansion, instead of His just simply commanding everything to happen automatically. He found it to be much more fun, to take His little brothers and sisters along for the journey. After all, He had gone to, and through, the cross, for each of us, just to make sure that we could have a Way to go with Him, forward into eternity.

After King Jesus had greeted everyone, and blessed them, He began to supernaturally show them all of the great wonders and delights which were being wrought continually. As it had been in the very beginning, now, these days, life, for everyone, had been transformed back into a steady flow of joy and delight, and every day and every night was filled again with wonderful and happy surprises. No one could ever surprise King Jesus, at least, not since Cornelius the Roman centurion had stunned Him one day early in His ministry, when Cornelius had claimed that Jesus had the power and authority to command his afflicted servant to heal, and that it certainly would happen! (The only reason that such a thing had caught King Jesus by surprise was that He had been intensely searching for faith in the people of Israel, not in Romans.) King Jesus had healed the servant of Cornelius that very hour, and had later sent Peter to Cornelius, as a reward for his excellent faith, to make him the first of all gentile converts! In this present time, Cornelius would have been made one of the great generals of the Army of Israel, except that Israel now only had an army of workers, and scientists, and builders. All of the enemies of the Lord had already been killed, or were finishing dying, in the lake of fire. From now on, war was just a fading memory, still taught to the children in school, as part of their history lessons, but no one ever wanted to fight anyone else these days. Everyone just fought to do right, and help King Jesus, and each other, to solve the design and construction problems with which they were dealing.

King Jesus showed them the rocket engine factory upon the moon, and showed them the test firing of the new gargantuan VASIMR rocket, which was mounted against a mountain upon the lunar surface, pointed outward into space. If the million-plus degrees did not have any atmosphere to disrupt, or any ecology to destroy, it was okay to fire it upon a surface, but not too forcefully, or for too long, so that it did not disrupt the orbit or rotation of the moon. (In extreme scenarios, yes, the huge engine could even affect the stability of a small planet.)

Everyone was overwhelmingly impressed, as the rocket did put on quite a show. After that, He showed them the factory where they were building the new space suits, and had a couple of the "moon people" walk around outside in the vacuum, and do all sorts of gymnastics, and back flips, and cartwheels, just so everyone could clearly understand that this was not their grandfather's spacesuit!

Then He showed them the factory where the sections of the titanium frames for the great ships were being grown, as huge, one-piece crystals, formed upon a strand of a magnetic field, which had been concentrated, and focused, until it acted like a single, one-inch thick, but absolutely unbreakable, strand of cable. The titanium formed around it, adhering to the specific shape, until a long section of frame tubing had been produced. The center was actually hollow, since that further reduced weight, and tubes are stronger than bars, anyway, since the tube behaves according to the principle of the Roman arch (actually, the Romans stole the idea from the Etruscans), distributing the stress, around the walls of the tube, instead of bending or breaking. Some of the sections being grown were over twenty miles long, and took several years to grow. After grown, they were forged with special radiation treatments, until the titanium was virtually indestructible.

King Jesus wanted everyone to know, and to participate, as much as possible, in the entire spectrum of projects which were being done. It was not only more fun for Him, it was exciting and fulfilling for all the people helping. It was good for everyone to have a chance to help Him, since no one would have even been still alive, if He had not saved them all.

After He had shown them all of the progress and developments up to the present, He promised them more wonders, yet to come, not yet known to any body else, except Him only, and told them to go home, rest for a Sabbath Year, and then get back to work. He blessed them, and told them how very pleased He was with all of them, every single person, and assured them all that each individual was going to play some very important part in the overall plan which He was unveiling. He reminded them that He had designed and built, and made work, an entire universe, and His projects, from now on, were going to be vast enough, and complex enough, so that everyone would have a chance to participate fully, if they wanted to do so. Either way, the projects would get done, the vision would come true, and the prophecies would all be fulfilled, in their own time!

The containment field, in which the plasma in the VASIMR rockets was controlled and directed, formed a shape like a long tube, or bottle, with the exhaust end opened up as the VASIMR fired. Even back in the old 20th Century, scientists had long been calling such a magnetic containment field a "bottle". Back in those days, no one had ever imagined that one day King Jesus would build a rocket big enough and strong enough to actually move worlds around. That's because no human mind could easily perceive just what the good Lord might consider a good size for one of His Own "bottle rockets". Now, that is fireworks, literally, done on a grand scale!

JUST ANOTHER BUNCH OF MIRACLES

Seven more wonderful years had passed, and they had brought astonishing growth, development, and increase. The moon factories were rolling along full bore, churning out mile after mile of forged titanium frame pieces for the great ships. Other factories there were making still more super monofilament cable for space elevators, since new ones would soon be installed upon Ahava and Lehaim.

The Earth itself was once again a lush, vast, overgrown jungle of fresh fruit, grains, and every possible kind of beneficial plant and herb. The animal world had also been restored, even stronger and more fully than it had ever been since the days of the Garden of Eden. All of the world's oceans were once again pure and clean, with just the right balance of salt and other dissolved chemicals, so that even all of the magnificent sea life, as well as the creatures which dwell in the fresh water lakes and rivers, had been restored, and the birds once more roamed the new air of the whole Earth.

They flew strong and free over mountains and seas that gleamed with the dazzling light of hope reborn, and dreams come true! They soared over endless green forests, and rainforests, and intense, deep jungles, and also open prairies, and far horizons of green fields, either growing, or being planted, or being harvested, depending upon the location upon Earth, and the local season. Seed time and harvest were still a foundational principle in the new Kingdom of Jesus Christ. Such things in the natural world were designed and built by Him to parallel the operational principles which are active within the spiritual realm, also.

He did this so that we could more easily understand His perfect Ways.

Peter, James, and John were sitting upon the main porch of the Temple. It was almost sundown, and it was the last night of Year 41. Sunrise would start Year 42, and this night would be the seventh-year festival celebration that had been held ever since the first time, which had been the evening before Year 7. The entire city of Jerusalem, and for that matter, the entire countryside all around there, was absolutely covered, with over a billion and a half people, since everyone in the world had to be present no later than sundown. People talked in low but excited voices, since everyone knew by now that these special Festivals always started off with a huge bang, and then got even more exciting from there!

The people of Earth had seen everything from new planets, miraculously formed right before their eyes, in a single night, to amazing space ships, moon factories, space elevators, and lunar mining operations, and a whole new design and application of incredible new rocket engines, which would easily drive the new ultra-ships between Earth and the brother planets, Ahava, and Lehaim. Everyone had made sure that they were there on time, for the start of the Festival, since, otherwise, they might miss some wonderful miracle, revealed for the very first time.

As the three apostles spoke together quietly, they discussed things shared only by the closest of the inner circle of the King. They nodded, smiled frequently, and once in a while, chuckled a bit at some inside joke or secret surprise, of which they knew, but which the good Lord had not yet shown to everyone else. As He had once done with His parables, He still chose to tell His closest friends His best secrets, first, and then share them later with all people. (He loved showing special honors unto those who especially honored Him.)

As sunset occurred, a mighty angel once again began the Festival, with an ear-splitting blast upon a huge shofar. He then announced the arrival of King Jesus Christ, as the good Lord instantly appeared high in the sky, right over the Temple. His sudden glory made everyone blink for a second or two, and then, unlike other previous occasions, the Lord did not diminish His glory, but, instead, He increased everybody's ability to see Him clearly, despite the dazzle, right through the intense glare of light.

Along with everyone else, the apostles bowed their noble heads, delighted to have Him there, and eager to see whatever He might show to them, this time.

As King Jesus smiled, He shouted, "Shalom!" All of the people also looked up and smiled back at Him, and shouted back, enthusiastically, "SHALOM!"

(Everybody laughed a bit, just at the general happiness of all of it all.)

The King then updated everyone about all the great progress and improvements, primarily upon Earth, and also upon the moon. Not only had the high speed trains continued to work flawlessly, upon both Earth and moon, but, now, the hydrogen-fueled internal combustion engine had been perfected. The main limitations in the old world had been how to store enough hydrogen onboard the vehicles to make it further than about 250 miles on a tank full of hydrogen. It had needed to be stored under high pressure, and this caused much hassle, and extra time for refueling, and extra weight for large, strong storage tanks.

The right answer had actually already been discovered, back in the old world, which had been cooking chicken feathers at a temperature of 750 degrees F, until the composition of the feathers broke loose, and the material expanded, which created tiny pockets in the fibers, which could and did store hydrogen molecules in much greater concentrations, and, at much lower pressures. The fuel cells for the new cars and trucks could easily hold enough hydrogen to drive the car, or truck, even 18 wheel sized trucks, all across the continent, on a single tank full of hydrogen, without having to stop to refuel, at all, until time to turn around, and go back.

The way the hydrogen produced motive power was not the same principle which had been employed with the gigantic (for the old world, anyway) rockets used for the moon shots, the legendary Saturn V. Those flying skyscrapers had used the hydrogen and oxygen, as direct fuel, and by burning the two together, in huge amounts, a thrust plume of over a thousand degrees was generated. Make it big enough, say, a flame of over fifty feet in diameter, and it could even lift and hurl a skyscraper into a 22,000 mile per hour orbit, or beyond, like the moon. Of course, the rocket had already shed stages one and two on the way up, so it was more the size of a small house, by the time it made it to orbit. (In fact, it was more the size of a small storage shed.)

The concept powering the personal vehicle, and the 18 wheeler alike, was electricity. They ran on high efficiency electric motors, direct-drive induction motors, where the rotor of the electric motor was the same as the drive shaft in the cars. Since magnetic suspension bearings had been perfected, and miniaturized, the motors ran friction-free, and could be accelerated astonishingly rapidly, and had virtually no upper speed limit, because of perfect balance, and no friction. By burning the hydrogen and oxygen, which was readily available in the Earth's atmosphere, an electric current was produced, which was what powered the electric motors. A very capable lithium-ion battery was incorporated, which was the buffer for the motor, to keep a steady power level. (The batteries were made right into the polycarbonate bodies of the cars and trucks, to save weight and space, and were an integral layer in the structure of the body panels, although the car bodies were all baked in one giant piece in the factory, and then doors and windows were cut into the shells later by lasers, and the interiors added, last.) The hydrogen just kept re-charging the battery at all times, faster than the motor could use up the battery charge.

The exhaust was only a bit of warm water vapor, more when the vehicle was under heavy load, or on a cold day, but it was usually just invisible, and quiet. That was extreme acceleration, extraordinary heavy-load capacity, cheap cost efficiency, low production costs (for such simple engines), low fuel costs, great reliability, and all with ZERO

EMISSIONS!! (Except for pure water vapor, that is.) Even the brakes used a dynamic braking system, where the energy used in slowing down the vehicle was also converted back into more electrical current, and also fed back into the main battery. Oil would have been used only for heating and lubrication, if these cars had been around in the 20th Century. There never would have been any sort of energy crisis, either, since the same precise principle could be applied to electrical power plants, to provide unlimited, almost cost-free, pollution-free, electrical power for cities and homes.

Hydrogen fills the whole universe. There is no place one cannot find hydrogen. That source of fuel can never run out, as long as the universe endures. By far, the more exotic and rare element of the two is oxygen, which is an oddity in the universe as a whole, but with which, we, upon Earth, have been supernaturally very blessed, indeed! We even have enough to breathe it!

The three apostles watched and listened, along with everyone else in the whole world, as King Jesus explained precisely how all these things were being done. Then, with a sudden flash of a smile, He paused, in the middle of His science lecture, and asked everyone, "So, tell Me, how do you like the new hydrogen cars and trucks, so far? Are they fun to drive?"

As soon as they heard the question, millions of Earth-people, the ones that had driven any of the new cars or trucks yet (since they had only been in production for a couple of years, now) leaped up to their feet, and jumped up and down, shouting things like, "Yea! Yea! Yea!" and, from the California Christians, "Far out, Man!" and from the forgiven and resurrected former oil company executives, and the old car company guys, "Well, better than nothing, I guess…"

King Jesus laughed at those sour buckets, and said, "Oh yeah? Just for that, I ought to make all of you guys walk everywhere!" He laughed at their sudden expressions of distress, and then returned to the lecture.

He resumed, "Now, you know all of the great progress and results which we have obtained upon Earth, and Moon. In fact, almost all of you had some major parts in at least some significant portion of the entire effort. Things are moving even better than we had scheduled. You remember from My Word that with Me, a thousand years is as a single day, and a day is as a thousand years. Well, I have expanded that framework, in two special cases, and, for each of our two new planets, I have accelerated the timeframe even further. For both Ahava and Lehaim, a million years, and, when necessary, even more, is as a single day, and a single day is as a million years. I placed this constraint upon those two planets, right at the start of Year 35, and since then, I have had the Cherub of Time, Gabriel, closely watching over, and supervising, the changes which we are producing there. The time it would normally take for us to terra-form two new worlds runs into the billions of years, but I wanted to have them ready for us to use, a lot sooner than that. So, at the rough equivalent rate of a day to a million years, over the last seven Earth years, over 2.5 billion years have passed, for each of the two new planets!"

He paused, for a long minute, to let all of that sink in, as all throughout the whole crowd, people murmured stunned, low comments like, "Whoa!" and "Wow" and, again, from the California Christians, "Far out, Man!"

People began to smile, as they suddenly realized the implications of His new revelation, and He smiled enormously, also, and threw His mighty Head back with a shout of a laugh, and said, "Yes, that's right! We are going to be able to begin settling the two new planets, sometime in this first century!"

Suddenly, the entire world, literally, exploded with wild shouts of excitement, and triumph, as if a long and painful war had just suddenly ended, with a great and total victory!

After about three or four minutes of uproar, King Jesus held up one hand, and everyone immediately fell quiet, listening eagerly. He continued, "We still have a lot of work yet to complete, but, at least, we can start the final preparation phase, a year from now, as soon as the Sabbath Year is done. Meanwhile, we are going to send 30 out of the fleet of 50 of the Earth-Moon rockets which we have now, since we need to send some of our new high-tech robots ahead to the new worlds, to begin construction of space ports, air ports, and, where needed, even sea ports."

"These are not what you might picture as a robot, like one of the human shaped monsters from the old science-less fiction of the old world. These are real, specialized machines, and some of them look like refrigerators, and some of them look like forklifts, and 30 of them even look like spaceships, and they are, too. I am sending machines, even though a lot of you are tough enough, now, as you have been growing stronger for decades, that you actually could walk around in vacuum, and survive radiation extremes, and severe cold, or heat. Even if you could, why just make you do something miserable, just to prove that you can? I already know that you would, if I asked you to do so."

"Another thing which is of critical importance is that we need to immediately seed all of both new worlds with grains, grasses, fruit trees, vegetables, herbs, and so on. Most of the flowers we will have to do a little later, once we have enough bees there to achieve the necessary levels of pollination. The hummingbirds will also help."

The view suddenly swung dramatically over to Lehaim, and it filled the sky, up close. People gasped in surprise. The planet was truly quite beautiful, in a strange, yet attractive way. Rather than a spectacle of mighty cliffs, deep gorges, enormous mountains, crashing waterfalls, or endless oceans, the people saw a planet with a landscape of large, swelling, rolling hills, and great wide, shallow basins, and large mesas, which rose out of gentle slopes from the surrounding flatlands. Lehaim had no rugged terrain anywhere, since it was originally the planet Mercury, which had been a molten slug of various metals and minerals, but which had never been allowed to cool off enough for any major landscape features, like mountains, to form and solidify, before they were melted down again into a mesa, or just a rise in the ground. Any crack or fissure which opened was instantly filled in with molten rock and iron, so it had been impossible for any sharp edges to form, anywhere. It would have looked like that upon Earth, if the whole planet had been essentially barely-cooled lava, which never cooled enough to form rugged terrain, jagged rocks, mighty mountains, or deep canyons. There were however many raw craters here and there, and this gave the surface a weird, almost lunar characteristic. Mercury had no atmosphere left, after the first Solar ignition, since the blast blew it all out to the asteroid belt. No atmosphere meant that asteroids could make it all the way down to the surface of Mercury, and slam into it, producing some impressive craters, but not as many or as massive as those upon the moon.

The effect upon the viewer was not one of boredom, but rather a strange peace and tranquility flooded the hearts of everyone, as their eyes followed the gentle swells and curves and contours of the newly cooled and solidified world, and people noticed large blue areas, which were the much smaller, but still vitally important, oceans of Lehaim. These oceans were not big, and they were not deep, but they were still oceans, all four of them, and they were about the size of the Great Lakes. A network of wide shallow rivers was already flowing all over the planet, and white cotton clouds skipped across a pure blue sky. The landscape was all colors, oranges, browns, reds, blues, purples, yellows, whites, blacks, grays, and many other shades and tones, but not a single green, anywhere on the whole planet. Somehow, the human heart ached for green, in any landscape, and the new planet looked dead and alien, without green. There were no birds, beasts, or fish, either. The oceans had been imported by means of comet strike, from special comets that King Jesus had reserved for now. They were almost all water ice, from the salvaged oceans of the original Mars. The world of Lehaim was named for life, but it was still a dead rock, until the Lord of Life touched it. He was just about to bring it to life, all over.

As the "camera" withdrew from Lehaim, people could clearly see the extensive aurora around the poles of Lehaim, fending off the deadly solar radiation, which would kill anyone as close as Earth orbit, if they were not reborn immortals. The magnetic fields of the new planets were just as important as atmosphere and oceans. Even if the new humans could handle a bit too much radiation, all of the other creatures, like animals, plants, and, of course, the newborn humans, still needed the full level of protection required.

Next, the view suddenly zoomed in upon Ahava, and everyone, even the people who knew what was coming, went numb with amazement, and shock, and stared with bugged out eyes, and dropped open jaws, unable to even think of any words to say. Peter said, in a whisper, "Wow, Lord!" James and John also looked up, silently overflowing with wonder, like everyone else.

The spectacle which had so stunned all of them into silence was a new, bold, absolutely breathtaking miracle of the Creator! They all saw a world much like Earth, with bright blue skies, big blue oceans, white puffy clouds, and much, much more. Unlike Lehaim, this world had dramatic variations in the topography. To call it "rough terrain" might well be a classic understatement.

The "camera" panned across the landscape, just below cloud level, and revealed a canyon big enough to span across the entire continental United

States! When the good Lord had combined the two planets, Mars, and Venus, He had saved a few of the distinctive features from each planet. The giant canyon, the grand canyon of Mars, was called Valles Marinus. Over three thousand miles long, and several hundred miles wide, it was just too special a feature to throw away. Now, a huge blue river was flowing noisily all through it, heading down to a vast ocean. Except for the total lack of green growing things, the monster canyon looked like the Earth's Grand Canyon, but as if growing on steroids, for about the last billion years!

As the "camera" continued to "fly" over the Valles Marinus, it reached the far end of the canyon, and, after following the large, widening river a bit further, it displayed a rather large ocean, at least by Ahava standards. The sea was about the size of the Mediterranean Sea on Earth. At the far end of the long ocean was a sight that made everyone "Wow!" even more.

Rising up through the cloud layers, the viewpoint shifted to reveal things hidden while at the lower elevations. Ahead of them loomed a gigantic wall of rock, several miles away, but stretching from right to left, completely blocking all further forward progress! The gray wall seemed to disappear up through the top of the sky, and was so tall and so wide that even the wide angle view of the "camera" could not see the stars above it, or anything at all to either side of it. It was just this overwhelming wall, slightly sloped back away from them, but only slightly. The upslope was so steep that it would have been difficult to try to drive up the wall with any present day vehicle.

As the "camera" continued to pull back away and up from the base of the wall, people could at last tell that it was more of a giant mountain peak, eventually narrowing to a pinnacle. It was a bright morning upon the base of the mountain, and there was no greenery yet upon it, but there was a snow line, which completely ringed the base, but stopped where the atmosphere, which was now identical to that of Earth, became too thin for water to form snow, or even ice. From there on up, much, much further, it was just dead, black rock, reaching up into the starry sky. The mountain actually reached from the flat surface of the planet, at sea level, all the way into space, beyond the atmosphere! (In fact, more than half of the monster was beyond the air, in the vacuum.) Any person standing upon the top of that mountain was just a short hop away from orbit.

"People of Earth, I give you Olympus Mons!"

The view then swung on past Olympus Mons, and showed the other three gigantic volcanoes from Mars, which had also been salvaged, intact. Also included in the planet-merge had been seven mountain ranges from Venus, and two additional very large, deep, and rugged canyons. Oceans were now a part of Ahava, and they had also been imported by means of ice-comet strikes, and the irony involved was that the original water oceans which had formed the ice-comets had been the huge oceans of Mars. Instead of the sailor coming home to the sea, this time, the seas came home to the planet! Ahava also had already formed large polar ice fields, storing reserves of fresh water as buffers for the world water supply there. The striking white ice at the top and bottom of Ahava looked very much like Earth's own poles. As the "camera" still continued to pull away and out into space, people could also see intense auroras at both poles, proving that the magnetic field was installed correctly, and up and running effectively around this new planet, also. People sighed as the view moved further out. They all wanted to go explore the new planets, especially Ahava!

"I know, I know, I am eager for us to be off to explore all of it, too! That's why we have been so hard at it for the last many years. Still, it will be done best with the right planning and preparation. For instance, to get this far, I had to finish stabilizing the internal structure of all three of the planets, including the Earth. I reached in and removed the "star without light" which is a quantum singularity, not an actual collapsed star. (Such things are sometimes produced when a supernova occurs, formed by warps and twists in the fabric of time and space around the supernova, because the amount of energy released is interacting in the space-time around it as though it were an enormous mass, like a giant black hole, if only for a few split seconds.) Remember, mass and energy cannot be created, or destroyed, at least, not by you, but only by Me. When a huge amount of energy is explosively released, the point source of that energy release is "seen" by the fabric of reality around it as something very heavy, with unimaginable gravity waves, insanely concentrated, and quantum black holes are knotted up into existence by the gravity waves. I had allowed this one into the center of the Earth, to achieve the changes I needed to produce in the structure of the Earth. It was the same one I used to split apart the Moon, and Mars, which used to be the same planet."

"Besides the internal structures of all three planets, they had to be finely calibrated at their O-2 and O-3 points, and perfected in their rotation and tilt. Every aspect of all of this has now been done, and we will launch the robot ships to the new planets, at sunrise. They are all loaded full with all of the things which I think they will need, like seeds, microbes, special terra-forming equipment, and so forth. The ships will land, at several selected places around each planet, in the temperate zones, near water, and begin to construct all of the start up structures we will need later, like space ports, housing, and so forth. The robots will also begin to set up seeding machines, which will roam by surface, and air, and water, all over the planet, spreading new seeds, of every kind of good, green, growing thing. You might have noticed that this time I did not see the need to bring back mosquitoes, fleas, or crabgrass. They served their purpose last time."

King Jesus looked to the east, and said, "Well, it's just about sunrise, so I will bid you farewell, and shalom, as we watch General Armstrong and his men conduct the launch sequence for all thirty rockets at once. We are also sending three additional rockets along to carry extra fuel, for all of the other rockets. If they run out, I will go bring them back Myself!"

"General Armstrong, are you and your people ready?"

"Yes, Sir, Lord!"

"All right! My people, may you enjoy your Year of Rest, because we are going to work even harder in the next six years after that, and maybe finally get this show on the road! Shalom!"

As He said this, all of the thirty three rockets fired at once, by pre-arranged orders, and the people of Earth watched in wonder, as thirty three streaks of hot blue fire leaped upward into the new dawn! As the trails of fire left the atmosphere, about half of them turned toward Lehaim, and the remaining group turned toward Ahava. The whole world cheered, as they vanished into the increasing morning glare. Then, people turned, and walked away to their own destinations, chatting excitedly about all they had just seen and heard.

Peter looked at his brother apostles, and said, "Boy, just when you think Jesus can't come up with anything grand enough to impress us any longer, huh?" He chuckled, and then he jumped, as he heard the rich, deep laugh of Jesus right behind him!

"So, I still have to work hard to impress you, Peter?"

"No, Lord, I was, as usual, just shooting off my mouth!"

Jesus looked Peter deep in the eyes, a twinkle of mirth dancing within, and He said, "I know. I know you also used your bold tongue to help Me to save a lot of people! I wanted you all to know that I am also impressed with each of you, too!"

JUBILEE ONE

Since it was going to be the seventh such Festival, everyone knew about what to expect. They all knew that they had to be within the traditional borders of Israel, no later than sundown, this day. Today was the last day of Year Number 48, and tomorrow began the Seventh Year, the Sabbath Year, of Year Number 49. This was indeed a very special year, since immediately after this year, came the Year Number 50, the Year of the Great Jubilee. There were certain special things that were part of a Jubilee Year, but, for tonight, everyone was just very excited about the Festival for Year 49.

Over the last 48 years, the population of Earth, and now, also the moon, had witnessed the miraculous creation of new planets, in a single night, and the conversion of a wrecked, dead Earth into a vital, pulsing, fruit-bearing, lush garden, a worldwide paradise, which had only been a memory and a dream of mankind ever since the Garden of Eden, up until now. The air was clean again, and so were the oceans, and the lakes, and the rivers. The greenery stretched from one end of the Earth, all the way unto the other. Most desert areas had been converted into vast new grain fields, and sparsely forested areas had been thickened intensely, and there were now several more rainforests, and deep jungles. Even parts of Antarctica had been sheltered under clear giant domes, just like the moon-domes, and were growing much food and other materials, like trees for lumber, all heated by geothermal spikes driven deep into the Earth, using the internal heat of the planet to keep the greenhouses at a steady 80 degrees. Human housing was also incorporated within these giant domes, and the frozen continent was finally being settled. Many giant mining tunnels had been bored into the rock there, and much gold and silver had been found, especially in the Norwegian section of the continent, which had once been attached to South Africa, and had many of the same mineral treasures, including vast deposits of excellent diamonds. Electrical power had to come from the same heat source used for warmth, but it was not any problem for the new technology. Just heat some water, from lots of free ice outside, hot enough until it turns into steam, and use the pressurized steam to turn turbine generators. More electrical power than that would never be needed, even if the entire continent were someday occupied.

Another reason for the interest in Antarctica was a similar idea as that about the moon. Some industrial processes can more easily and swiftly be achieved, if the temperature is very cold, say as in Antarctica. Some special items used in the new high tech machines and vehicles could be made at the South Pole, just as well, and much more cheaply, than in the lunar factories.

As the sundown began, the people all began to talk, in low, but very eager and excited whispers. What would He show them this time? How would He top all of the magnificent wonders which He had already produced, right before their own eyes?

All eleven of the original apostles, and Mathias, and Paul, were gathered at the porch of the Temple. Also, for this special Year, standing near to them were the prophets, from Abel, all the way to John the Baptist. Mingled in amongst those mighty men of faith were the other legendary heroes of the whole Bible, including the forgiven (like everyone else, and fully resurrected) Adam and Eve, Enoch, Noah, Job, Daniel, as well as all of the decent kings of Israel. (Some of them had been too evil to save.) Alongside of the kings, stood, equal in honor, all of the mighty men of war, of the Lord, all of the way from Seth, Noah, Job, Abraham, Israel, Joseph, Moses, Joshua, Caleb, Gideon, Samson, David, Solomon, Uriah, Hezekiah, Josiah, Nehemiah, the Maccabees, and many others, less known to history, but well known unto the good Lord, all the way to modern era soldiers of Israel. These included Ariel Sharon, Ehud Barak, and the Netanyahu brothers, as well as many from the time of re-establishment, right after World War II. Alon Galal, Imi Lichtenfield, Moshe Dayan, and many others less famous were there, and also Theodore Herzl. There was a man there also whose name no one knew, but somehow, everyone knew clearly that he had been once known as the "thief on the cross" who died alongside Jesus. In this world, he was famous everywhere he went for this one thing, when he had confessed his faith in our good Lord, while hanging next to Him, upon his own well-deserved cross. Maybe his faith had even encouraged Jesus, to stay tough all the way through the cross, until He beat it.

As the sky grew darker, suddenly, a great cherub appeared upon the porch of the Temple. His splendor was stunning, when seen up close and personal like this. A cherub was such a mighty, moving tower of goodness, that to be near one was to be reminded of absolute purity, at a level so powerful, and profound, that it shook the very bone marrow. His great feet were upon the porch, but his great shining head was a couple of miles up in the night sky, and his wings stretched far out over the crowd, and all of them were gasping in surprise and wonder! Their hearts raced with excitement and their pulses thundered within them!

The cherub lifted the largest shofar in the universe, which was the same one he had used upon command from King Jesus, to signal the Seventh Trump, when, after the Tribulation, all of the saints, those still alive upon the Earth, and those buried in the Earth or sea, were raised and gathered together with King Jesus Christ, in the high upper atmosphere, on a bright beautiful morning!

Gabriel blasted forth a practically solid wave of sound out of the shofar, which shook the ground under them. Still, for all its' intensity, the note was pure and clear, lovely, and did not even hurt their ears, although it penetrated even the solid rock of the whole Earth. As he lowered the shofar, he said, "I am Gabriel: that stands in the Presence of Almighty God! I am the Chief Herald for the Son of God!"

As he took another deep breath, the people stood transfixed, in anticipation.

Gabriel pointed his arm straight up, looked straight up, and roared, "BEHOLD OUR KING!"

Instantly, an overpowering flash of ultra-white light dazzled everyone's eyes, but, as they blinked, they began to perceive the good Lord Jesus Christ, suspended in the air over their heads, another two miles or so higher, and He appeared even much taller than Gabriel. The Wings of the Lord stretched way out far, covering the whole central region of Israel! He looked down and all around at everyone, and somehow, His majestic Eyes seemed to briefly touch each person's own eye's, and to reach gently deep into each heart. Everyone listened and watched very attentively, feeling as though the good Lord were talking to only him, and not to every one else, too.

King Jesus smiled happily, and shouted, "SHALOM!"

The entire world, and everyone in it, including the little babies, responded, "SHALOM!" (Even the animals listening answered, as they were best able.)

As soon as King Jesus had spoken, Gabriel had quietly vanished, and all that the people could see was the brightly glowing King Jesus, the stars, and the ghost of the new moon in the background.

King Jesus spread out his wings and arms wide over all of them, and said, "You are all, each one of you, blessed indeed, for this is the Festival to celebrate our seventh seven-year Sabbath, and immediately next is the First Jubilee! We will observe the Sabbath Year as usual, but, in the Year 50, we will do something special, which is now possible because of the advanced state of our technology, and all of the extra help we have from machines and robots. We will still have a spring planting next year, even though it is a second Sabbath Year, being a Jubilee, but we will have all the planting, tending, harvesting, processing, and distribution done by machines and robots, instead of people. Instead, people will be tending to other business, such as restoring family lands to one another, clearing and forgiving debts, releasing bonds, and restoring people to their rightful dignity, although, in this age, nobody should have too many wounds or debts to worry about, if any. Nonetheless, we will still observe the Jubilee, every 50 years, since I ordained it as a statute forever, throughout all of your generations. When Yom Kippur arrives, not this one, but the one for year 50, you will all hear Gabriel sound his shofar again, from the Temple porch, and I will proclaim the Year of Jubilee. No matter where you are, resting and worshipping, that Day, you will hear the shofar, at noonday, and you will immediately hear My Voice issue the Proclamation!"

"When you hear that, begin your final preparations, those of you which will be applicants for transfer, to the new planets. Those of you selected will then undergo extensive further training, and heavy conditioning, since settling a new world requires strength, and much stamina. Your training will last about a half a year. Then we will begin final stocking of the Ark II. I encourage individuals without families, or else, whole, entire families, to apply. I do not wish to split any family units apart, not even for the greatest adventure possible!"

After He had said this, many people murmured excited, low conversation snips throughout the crowd, as everyone wondered if they should be one of the applicants. After a few moments, King Jesus continued.

He went on to tell them about all of the extensive and ultra-successful progress which had been completed upon the Earth, and the fully operational moon industries, which were nearly finished with the Ark II. The final phases were being completed by robot's labor, as the humans stopped for the Sabbath Year. He assured them that everything would be ready precisely on time.

Then He smiled, and said, "Now, we come to a part of this evening's Festival, that I have waited long to show you. You do recall that I changed the time rate for the new planets, so that the progression requiring billions of years could be actually achieved, by the time we wanted to go there. Last Festival, we sent out the robots in rockets, to begin what we wished, for the preparation stages to facilitate our settling of these new worlds. I dialed back the time-warp there, so each of the new planets reverted to the rate of a day equals a thousand years. That means, mathematically, that about 2,550,000 years have effectively passed upon the new planets, while our robot army has been hard at work all that time, building, planting, and installing things, which include many high speed trains, mining tunnels, space ports, airports, seaports, and so forth. Also, remember that I told you that I was going to prepare a place for you. Well, I am about finished, having made these ready for use, and so I will now show you just why you might want to consider applying to move there!"

Suddenly, the sky scene was filled with Lehaim, as the "camera" zoomed in close to it. People saw a lush green planet, with moderate-sized, light blue oceans, and many wide, slow rivers, and thousands of shallow lakes, and endless expanses of green fields and forests, and much of the terrain even appeared to be plowed into rows. Nowhere was there seen any square, sectioned off piece of ground, such as the farmlands had shown upon old Earth. All of this planet, and everywhere else, was owned by One Person, although He freely shared it with everyone else. He did allow personal property, but would not ever again let people carve up His land into little square, unnatural packages. If someone

wanted a boundary to his farm, he just
better choose someplace where a natural
boundary already existed, although
fences of any kind, except for decorative
hedges around the homes themselves,
were absolutely prohibited. No one was
allowed to brand or kill any animals any
more, either. From now on, the animals
would always have their own freedom
and dignity guaranteed, and if anyone
tried to think otherwise, the animal
himself spoke up, and the person,
immediately chastised, would stop
whatever old habit he was trying to
wrongfully start again. People in this age
had their hearts right with God, and did
not want to hurt the animals, or any thing
else that lived. Instead, everyone wanted
to obey and please the good Lord.

Because many people had learned to
love meat in the old Earth, the good Lord
had developed a cloning technology, the
like of which would have been the envy
of every genetic scientist in the world, in

the old days. Cell samples were taken and cultured, and processed perfectly, then shaped correctly, so that now you could still enjoy a fine steak dinner, but no animals had to suffer or die to make it possible! (All of the clean meats were available, but there were no pigs of any kind in these new days, so no one could eat pork of any sort, even if he wanted to do so.)

Even so, people still liked other things, like milk, and cheese, and eggs, so, many farm animals were still kept, but only if they did not mind staying there willingly on the farm. Somehow, they understood, deep in their little hearts, no one would ever kill or hurt them any more. This innate, Divinely granted knowledge, made them want to hang around the farm and give milk, eggs, and cheese. The horses and other work animals, including all of Donkey's sons and daughters, never had to do any more hard work, forever, but they could come and go as they wished. Somehow, enough of them always seemed to volunteer to provide for the needs of the farm families. Most of the people of Earth had moved away from cities, to live on small farms, all over the planet. Some just liked to wander around, living as nomads. This was easy, since food was exceedingly plentiful everywhere they went, except in the frozen areas.

As the view zoomed in yet further, the people all gasped at the loveliness of this planet, which had once been dead Mercury. The whole thing was a gently curving panorama of lush green hills, vast open plains, beautiful, calm beaches, and everywhere they looked, there were the faint, well-concealed, tracks of the high speed trains, laid out so as to blend in with the natural contours of the terrain. There were cities, seaports, airports, very many high speed trains, even two space elevators, and just about everything else people could use or need to live comfortably. In the cities, there were millions of the hydrogen burning, non-polluting cars and trucks, all brand new, parked and ready to drive, lined up in vast parking areas, and all along the streets of the cities.

All of the people, the very young, and their grandparents alike, "ooohed" and "aaahed" and went, "Oh, wow!" There was just one beautiful, peaceful scene after another, all over the whole planet.

The good Lord spoke again, after letting them all see and contemplate the calm beauty of the special pastoral world, a place for peace and calmness. He said, "I am glad you like it! I like it, too, but it will be very much better, once some people and animals are there, also, to make it come to life! For some of you, this will be the place you wish to call your new home, from now on, although, of course, you can move back to Earth, if you ever want to do that. By the way, all of the time warps are now de-activated, so we can accurately interact with our robot friends, as we travel there, so the schedules are consistent."

The King spoke again, "If that is a little too tame for your tastes, and you prefer a more intense landscape, maybe you will choose Ahava!"

As He said that, the view suddenly was filled with a planet so rugged, raw, and wild, that it both stirred the heart, and quickened the breath, as soon as they saw it! The sharp, savage beauty of all of it took them by surprise.

They had seen the topography of both Lehaim, and also, Ahava, but the one missing color in the chromatic scheme of both planets had been green. Light green, dark green, and all shades of in-between green had now been painted all over everything, wherever plants could grow and thrive. When King Jesus had shown them Lehaim, the green had so well blended into the scenery, none of them had noticed, or remembered, that seven years earlier, the planet had been red, orange, and everything but green. This time, Lehaim had just seemed somehow completed, and just looked right.

When they saw Ahava, the greenery here made dramatic statements. In sharp contrast against snow-blanketed peaks, and also in distinct variance with the deep, deep blue of this planet's saltwater oceans, which were much, much deeper than those upon Lehaim, here, the green colors completed the picture, as well, but in far more stunning fashion. Lehaim was designed for farmers, and fresh water sailors. Ahava was designed, instead, for mountain climbers, white water rafters, deep ocean divers, surfboarders, skydivers, and so forth. The only prohibited wild sport upon Ahava would be hunting, or fishing. Cloned food made such things obsolete, as peace had done to war!

While the people had been impressed, and very pleased with Lehaim, even so, wild cheers, and shouts of joy, erupted from those more adventurous souls amongst them, as they saw the planet which had, literally, been made just for them! All of them knew instantly, as to whether they would choose Lehaim, Ahava, or remain upon the Earth. Many of them began to chant, "Ahava, Ahava, Ahava, Ahava!"

King Jesus smiled, then held up a hand, so they would calm down a bit. He then continued, "Do not worry, any of you that wish to go to either of the two new worlds will ultimately be allowed to do that, but, for now, we will select our most viable candidates for the Ark II. The pioneers will have a lot of work to accomplish, but, given a little time, we will have both planets available and optional for everyone that wants to visit them, or even move there. We have plenty of room, with three whole worlds, don't you think?"

Everyone shouted "Yes!"

King Jesus continued, "Notice that here, as we view Ahava, the trees are a lot of the giant redwoods, sequoias, and lodge-pole pines. The vegetation of this rugged world will match the terrain, as with Lehaim. Also, the animals which will be stocked here will be the wilder, stronger, more rugged beasts, in keeping with the rough terrain. Notice the extensive arctic regions, which will be filled with arctic animals, too. Look, see Olympus Mons?"

The view swung across the landscape to the gigantic volcano mountain, and they saw how breathtaking the raw, savage wonder appeared, with dark, thickly forested lower slopes, that covered the base, all the way up to the snow line. From there up, the snow painted the mountain pure white, until the point where the air grew too thin to have precipitation, which never had happened upon Earth, but this mountain towered beyond the atmosphere, and the upper part was jet black, except the part where the direct sunlight hit it, which was a dark gray, all the way to the peak.

King Jesus spoke again, while they were all watching, stunned into wonder, and silence, by the spectacle. He said, "Look, that's not the only one!"

Then the "camera" panned out to show three additional great, extinct volcanoes, also reaching up beyond the atmosphere, but not as high. All of them were beautiful.

There were other, rugged mountain ranges, all over the whole planet, and many of them had been salvaged from Venus. One particular range had almost straight up vertical walls and cliffs, and stood about as tall as the Himalayas. The extreme heat and temperature upon Venus had allowed the rocks to form and hold much more solid, dense, unbreakable mountains, as the rock material was essentially slow-cooked for millions of years, until it was like forged steel. Earth had never had mountains as big as the great volcanoes, or as rugged as the imports from Venus.

Then the sky-picture vanished, leaving everyone blinking, as King Jesus said, "Now, I have just shown you what I, and the cherubs, and the angels, and our robots have been producing for you. Next, let Me show you what men and robots have been producing to fit into the picture perfectly!"

As He said this, the view was suddenly full again, with a view of the curve of the moon's surface, and, several miles up into space, in synchronous orbit, floated a marvel they had not seen yet, except for the men and women that had been working upon it. Suspended by centrifugal forces, and moored to Tototus, the moon's space elevator anchor, floated a vast, shiny new spaceship! It gleamed in the raw sunlight, and overwhelmed the senses, as people began to grasp just how enormous the thing really was. From one end to the other, it stretched almost 100 miles! In diameter, it measured over 12 miles! The entire hull was clear, see-through plastic, made from carbon nano-fiber, grown into form as one giant crystal, grown right onto, and made part of, the tubular titanium framework. The monster was far too massive to ever land upon a planet, but the VASIMR rocket on board was strong enough to launch it again, if it ever needed to do so. As the view zoomed in closer and closer, all they could see was the great, clear wall of the ship's hull, automatically reflective on the sun side. After zooming in a long time, they were finally able to make out tiny little machines, which were robots, scurrying all over the ship. They were finalizing the assembly and calibration of everything upon the great ship, and even though they looked tiny, some of those robots were larger than an Abrams tank. The largest robot was about the size of a World War

II battleship, and it moved carefully along the outer surface of the hull, making final treatments and adjustments upon and within the hull structure, so everything would be absolutely flawless, long before launch.

People watching were laughing in delight, shouting in excitement, crying tears of extreme joy, and literally jumping up and down, pounding each other on the backs in excitement, with everyone hugging everyone else, and starting to go wild, as they might in the old world, at a New Year's party. King Jesus smiled, as He looked with great love, down upon all of them, and then He said, "Okay, so now you can see that we are almost ready, and it has all turned out as we had hoped! So, now that you know what the options are, go home, read up more details about it, if you wish, and discuss all these things with your family members, and by the time 18 months have passed, it will be Yom Kippur, the

Day of Atonement, Year 50, and I will proclaim the First Jubilee! Those who wish to go, and have been approved, will then report to the Pioneer Training Center, here in Jerusalem, and, about five and a half months later, when you have completed your training and certifications, we will load the Ark II with all of the people and animals we are taking to Ahava. The journey will take about ten weeks one way. Once there, off loading will commence, and everyone and everything, except for the robots, and the pilot crew, will be brought down to the surface by space elevator. Locations for recommended settlement will be listed at the space ports, so you can pick which high speed train route you want, and print out and download maps and other technical data which you will want. Hiking and camping supplies are already stocked, at all of the train depots, so, just grab what you want to take on the way out. Anyway, more about all that stuff, later! For now, go home, rest, get ready, and then, be back on time to go."

"Now I bless each of you, in the Name of the Father, the Son, and the Holy Spirit! Go in peace. Shalom!"

After King Jesus said this, He suddenly vanished, leaving everyone blinking again, for a few seconds. Then, they all turned, and began to make their ways home. Some were deep in thought, especially those with families, but the young and single folks were afire with wild enthusiasm and excitement, and chattered on with each other about just what they wanted, and planned, to do. Now, King Jesus had given them all some very powerful, and strange, new things of which to dream.

They did rest that Year, and then tend to the business required by Jubilee Law, and then, upon the 10th Day of the Seventh Month of the Jubilee, Gabriel appeared again upon the Temple porch, and sounded the great shofar, and everyone clearly heard King Jesus proclaim the Year of Jubilee! Those with hearts set for departure said their good-byes, and headed for Jerusalem. Once there, they were quickly screened, and selected, or told to apply for a later flight. The chosen were then taken into intense training, and kept there for about five months. One week before the end of the Year of Jubilee, the loading of all people and animals commenced, and continued around the clock, for six days. Then, the last Saturday morning in the Year of Jubilee, King Jesus suddenly was clearly heard by everyone in the whole world, as He declared, "Now, people of My Kingdom, look up, and cheer for our brothers and sisters, and the animals, too, as they depart for Ahava!"

Everyone, all over the Earth, whether it was day or night, whether they were indoors or out, obediently looked up straight over head. By miraculous arrangement, everyone was enabled to watch, as the great vessel drifted loose from its' moorings, and moved out further into space, away from Totutus, moved by centrifugal force.

As they watched, captivated, a sharp blue spear of intense fire shot out from the rocket end of the ship, lighting up all of the Totutus side of the moon, brighter than the lunar sunrise, as the mighty VASIMR rocket roared to life. No one heard any sound, however, since there was no atmosphere present to convey sound. Even so, the intense energy released by the VASIMR sent rumbles of shock and vibration even across the intervening space, and people upon the moon could feel the faint trembling of the lunar surface under them, like a very, very mild moonquake. Totutus was shaken much more, being much closer, but this had been foreseen, and everything that was vulnerable upon the station had been removed beforehand, including all flesh bodies. (Even children of light would not want to be too close to a huge VASIMR, whenever it fired off.) The people and animals onboard the ship had special shielding, which effectively prevented any damage or harm to any of them. Intense magnetic fields forced the heat and radiation out into the exhaust of the rocket, so they were very, very safe on board.

The entire world watched, as the behemoth seemed to hang motionless, for about three seconds, and then began to inch slowly away from the moon. As greater distance was achieved, the rocket began to really open fire, and the giant ship began to rapidly accelerate. After about six or seven seconds like this, it suddenly brightened even more, and the ship faded into the night sky like a dragster leaving the lights! All they could see then was an intense, tiny point of ultra-bright blue light.

Everyone in the whole world was cheering, laughing, crying, many of them screaming shouts of joy and celebration, and just generally going berserk! As the tumult began to settle down, they all heard King Jesus say again in their minds, "Now, Admiral Noah and his crew will be back after they drop off the settlers for Ahava, in about another five months. During that time, we will screen and accept people for departure to Lehaim. Those selected will also undergo the training, and then, we will reload the Ark II, and send it to Lehaim, with another load of people and animals. We will make as many flights as we need, but will hold it down to about one flight a year after these first two. (We have to maintain all of the equipment, and also the people involved need to rest in between missions for a little while, and go home to visit their families between flights.) So, in order to be ready when Noah and the Ark II return, those of you which wish to move to Lehaim, please leave for Jerusalem immediately, the morning after tomorrow. Today is a Sabbath, the end of the Jubilee, so, rest, and tomorrow, pack your bags, and then come to Jerusalem for preparation."

King Jesus suddenly stopped, and said, "Noah, is everything onboard all right?"

Instantly, everyone heard Noah's voice, and they somehow knew it was his voice, as he replied, "Aye, Lord! Ship-shape, as it might be said!"

They all heard the Lord chuckle at that, as He replied, "Well done! Godspeed and blessing upon your journey! Call Me, if you need anything, or even if you just want to talk."

Then, He directed His comments to everyone, as He said, "Okay, five more years, until the next Seven Year Festival. Meet Me in Jerusalem, the last night of Year 56, no later than sundown, and then I will show all of you what new surprises I have made for you, so that you may marvel! SHALOM!"

A MAN OF HIS WORD

Nine hundred and fifty years is quite a long time. A whole lot can happen in human history, in that long a span. For instance, start at the Battle of Hastings, in 1066, and end with Space Stations and Space Shuttles, in the early 21st Century. The dramatic impact, and extreme extent, of such "changes over time" can be even further intensified, if those years are occurring during the 1,000-year Millennium, when King Jesus rules the whole Earth, and other worlds, as well, and peace is always enforced, forever, by mighty angels and cherubs. There is another, even more effective Way, in which peace is enforced, forever. The love of God is now present, forever, in every person, and any other type of creature, welded into every living heart. No one, and no thing, wants to do anything wrong, or hurt anyone else.

Adam and Wolf had resumed their ancient chase and tag games with Horse, and they all played once again, as before the disaster of sin. The original creatures, almost every one of them (except the serpent!), as well as the original humans, had been restored unto the Garden of Eden, which had been completely rebuilt and re-seeded, and re-populated, with every one, and every thing. Now, things were, again, as before sin, except for the change that the humans now wore clothing, and also, that the humans now knew enough, about the knowledge of good and evil, that they never wanted to know anything more about evil, in any form, or any tiny amount, no matter what, forever!

In the last 950 years, King Jesus had directed the resurrected, and also the newborn, human race, on three densely populated worlds, to greater and grander projects and developments, all of which proceeded at ultra rapid pace, being designed, managed, and funded by Him. Even special time-warps, time rate changes, and such other extraordinary things were not ruled out, when it came to the King finishing His projects correctly, and in His time.

After the first voyage of the Ark II, many more followed, and soon, millions of people were living, working, playing, and thriving upon both Lehaim, and also Ahava. The vast advanced systems and infrastructure installed by robots had greatly expedited the settlement and growth of both of the two worlds.

The population increases had never stopped, on any of the three worlds, and so, the Lord had invented, and had men install, a very different type of space elevator. This one was anchored to a gigantic, floating platform, which was a square platform, five miles on a side. Twenty five square miles of titanium, steel and floats was enough mass to hold the Earth end of the cable as well as a deeply anchored rock-anchor cable. The entire platform was slightly submerged, being constructed of tubular titanium, and only the floats and the cable showed above the water, except for the flashing warning lights all around the edges of it, sticking high above the water on carbon-fiber poles. Where the cable emerged from the sea, at the very center of the framework, many large magnetic field generators shaped a column of magnetic force, which acted as a starter guide, for a permanent water spout, a funnel cloud of water, not dirt, as an artificial tornado lifted the water up from the sea, and guided it along the cable, accelerating it upward, by charging the water molecules, and then driving them up at near-light speed, in similar fashion as a particle accelerator, but on a monumental scale, so that a twisting column of sea water was continually being rammed into space. At the top of the cable, another large asteroid anchored the collectors, and storage tanks, and pump stations which gathered the water as super heated vapor, still charged, into condensed, but not quite frozen, liquid water minus all of the salt, and other chemicals, which had been stripped away while accelerating upwards, as the water was vaporizing into high velocity steam. When the tanks were filled, one of the huge fleet of Ark ships came and filled up its' onboard storage tanks, and off they went, to drop much more water upon the young oceans of Ahava, and Lehaim. Increasing population meant increasing need for more water sources, even with the extremely effective water management systems in use in this new Way of life.

The Earth had always had plenty of sea water to spare, anyway, and now, under the leadership and wisdom of King Jesus, all water resources were being managed correctly, and people and animals could get more and better results, without so much excess sea water. In the centuries that had passed, the Earth's oceans had been reduced by about half, and the sea level had been deliberately lowered, so that the continental shelves all were exposed to the air now, and these areas were all being planted with crops, and settled intensely, since people still needed to be near whatever oceans were left. It also meant that, even though one could still sail all around the Earth, it had to be done in a more restricted fashion, instead of just striking out across an endless expanse of ocean. Now, one had to follow deep channels, wherever the oceans still were sailable. The increased land area still had lots of water imbedded within it, except that it was stored more effectively, in green, thriving grass, grains, bushes, and large trees. The oceans upon the other two planets had been dramatically increased, since the transfer of water had been continuing for centuries. Now, the Earth looked more like a big green and white marble (white clouds), with blue highlights, instead of the old "big blue marble".

All of the changes and improvements had not been limited to the planets, only. The good Lord had sent out men and angels to find and retrieve special mineral rich asteroids, scattered far and wide in the asteroid belt. Even with VASIMR rockets, it still took months to get out to the asteroids, so the payload had better be worth all the effort. The asteroids they brought back were essentially small planets of almost pure metals and gemstones, with diamonds bigger than football stadiums, emeralds the size of small ships, rubies as big as 18 wheelers, and literally mountains of silver, gold, titanium, magnesium, chromium, platinum, uranium, and just about any other type of mineral treasure one might wish. The asteroids were the shattered and frozen remains of the outer shells of the inner planets, and now there were only the rocky cores that remained, which had been made into the three worlds. Those outer shells had still been thousands of miles thick, just before the Sun ignited, and the explosive force of that light-up had sent most of the solid material fragments from the inner planets out as far as the region where they now orbited, as asteroids. They had kept buried within them all of the rich minerals that had once been part of their planets of origin. Now, it was time to harvest those riches!

Along with all of the exploration and settlement happening upon the inner planets, missions had also been built and sent to begin settlement of some of the large moons of the gas giant planets, such as Jupiter and Saturn. A lot of the material in the rings of Saturn was actually H_2O, and those ice chunks could be collected and sent to the new worlds, to further help build up the new oceans. Titan and Ganymede were the first two moons, of the gas giants, which were explored, since their gravity was much like that of the Earth, and that made it much easier to build shelters, and then live and work there. Some things could be done well in free fall, but, for some things, a solid platform and about one Earth G were just needed, for proper operations. One cannot pour a glass of water, in space.

The good Lord Jesus did not restrict His space-settlement plans only to the Earth, or just the Earth, plus two more planets. No, He carried the theme out much further. He had designed, and had built, giant interstellar ram ships, which were launched by giant VASIMR booster rockets, until accelerated up to a fraction of light speed, at which point, far-reaching powerful magnetic fields were extended out ahead of the ships, which acted like scoops, gathering and compressing interstellar hydrogen, which fills the entire Universe. (No matter how empty space may seem, there is still a lot of hydrogen, everywhere, out there.) When the hydrogen is forced into the combustion chamber of the onboard fusion rocket, and the heat from the VASIMR exhaust is used to ignite it, the ongoing, sustainable fusion rocket fires up, and off to the stars we go! Even with all of that, a journey to Alpha Centauri still took about forty years, 20 years of acceleration, then flip the ship around, and 20 years of hard negative acceleration, or, as some call it, deceleration, during which the magnetic scoop fields were angled backwards, at a very wide angle, since the ship was then flying backwards, but hydrogen still had to be collected for fuel. The wide angle gathered enough hydrogen, without inhaling the rocket exhaust accidentally. The final result was the ship arriving in orbit around Alpha Centauri. That was not the only target, either. A ship was also dispatched unto Sirius, about twice as distant as Alpha Centauri. The ships did not have living creatures onboard, except in the form of seeds for grass and trees, and frozen microbes, of the types which helped to convert a planet's atmosphere from toxic to breathable. Even if people had been aboard, the magnetic shields would have protected them from the fusion radiation, which was forced out back, along with all the heat and thrust. When the ship reversed, and flew backwards, additional extra-strong magnetic fields shunted all of the radiation and heat plume away from the cabin and payload section.

The ships were flown, and staffed, by many different types of specialized robots. Their assignment was to find the specific worlds which the good Lord had set there for them, and begin terra forming them, with the ultimate goal to make them human-habitable, in preparation for settlement. Since the ignition process which had produced the exposed rocky cores of our own inner planets occurred with every star, there were many more Earth-sized worlds out there, all about in the same orbital range, and our own old world science had just not been able to see them, all those light years away. One day, the children of light would walk without space suits, on strange worlds, under strange suns. There was still much work to be done, first.

Everyone in the whole Earth, and everyone everywhere else, including Ahava, Lehaim, the moon, all of the space stations and space elevators, and even out at the moons of the outer planets, was required to be at least "electronically present and accounted for", no later than sunset, in Jerusalem, Earth, on the evening of the last day of Year 998. The next day was the first day of Year 999, and it would be a Sabbath Year, of rest, and it was to be followed immediately by Year 1,000, and the Grand Jubilee, marking the end of the first thousand years of the reign of King

Jesus Christ! None of the people there watching, in Jerusalem, or wherever they were, geographically, even on remote worlds, could even begin to guess what amazing spectacle that the good Lord might have prepared to overwhelm them, but they all knew that it would be something very huge, and astonishing! Everyone grew quiet, and watched and listened, very attentively, as the evening sky deepened a bluer blue, and became black night.

Suddenly, Gabriel appeared in blazing splendor, and raised his tremendous shofar, and sent forth a pure note of joy, and also a battle call, all rolled into one, as if the giant shofar were delighting to play the cavalry charge, eager to rush into combat! The Earth, and all of the other planets, shook when he sounded the note. As he lowered the horn, he raised his great arm, and pointed almost straight overhead, and roared, "BEHOLD OUR

KING, JESUS CHRIST: HE IS THE HOLY SON OF GOD!!!"

As he said this, he vanished, and all the blinking people everywhere could see was a small, white-hot point of light, growing rapidly larger, and much, much brighter, until everyone was squinting and straining to see through the glare of light. As the bright spot grew closer at frightening speed, they began to make out the shape of a great winged thing, so bright that seeing details was still impossible.

Suddenly, the glare began to reduce, as if done automatically, and everyone could instantly see clearly that the winged thing was Tzedek-Sus, the Mighty War Horse of King Jesus! Seated upon His horse was the Son of God, blinding in His shining glory. His Face was like the Sun at noonday, and His Eyes were like hot, white lasers. If the people had not all, each one of them, known that He knew and loved every one of them, they would have been terrified. Even so, they still became a little nervous, at the sheer magnitude of His power and majesty. After all, He and Tzedek-Sus filled the whole sky, and seemed somehow to stretch a little beyond its' edges, too! They each had great white wings which stretched beyond the limits of the eye to see, and the tips of their wing feathers faded into infinite distance to each side. The blazing crown of King Jesus seemed to scrape the ceiling of Heaven! Everyone gasped involuntarily, stunned by His full appearance, which He usually reduced, so people could stand to look Him in the Eye, and talk with Him.

He and Tzedek-Sus came skidding to a thundering halt, actually seeming to kick up stardust, somehow. He let His horse rear up, and after a paint-peeling scream, when the horse settled down again, the King looked around at all of them, and smiled, and shouted, "SHALOM!"

All of the creatures in all of the worlds shouted back "SHALOM!"

He smiled even more, and said, "Welcome, to the 140th Seventh Year Sabbath Festival! Tomorrow is the first day of Year 999, which will be a year of Sabbath rest. Immediately after this Sabbath Year, we will have the Grand Jubilee, which will be Year 1,000, and will mark the end of the first thousand years of our new lives!"

As He said this, all of the people everywhere cheered wildly. He then went on, "What I require of you is to observe the usual things this Sabbath year, and then, at the start of the Grand Jubilee, you will have one month to complete all of the usual Jubilee business. After that you will have only five months left to completely move yourselves, and all of your belongings, totally clear of the Middle East. From the Black Sea, to the Red Sea, and from the Mediterranean to the Caspian, you must vacate entirely.

Anything left there will be lost, and destroyed forever. Do not leave behind even one of your pets, if you wish to still have them around. You will each obey Me in this, perfectly. Do not be late getting everything out!"

Then He spent the next few hours recounting with them all of the great projects and adventures they had all shared, reminding them how everyone had played an important part, and they could all be proud of what had been achieved, and the best part was how everyone had grown so very much closer over the last 998 years, and how they now knew and loved each other with full knowledge, and deep respect, as they never could have done in the old world. The greatest thing built over the thousand years was a healed, complete human race, without contentions or hurts against anyone. About the roughest it got was when people bet a month's worth of yard mowing against each other, when they were watching the slow motion races of the competing space yacht entries from each world, racing strange, small ships across the gap between worlds, driven by solar wind from the Sun, pushing huge sunlight-capturing sails. The races began in the spring upon Earth, but were not finished until autumn. The ships all launched from orbit around Ahava, and headed for Earth, as it sped toward them, racing in its' orbit around the Sun, right behind Ahava. Since Earth was moving at them at 70, 000 miles per hour, the yachts had to plan their path to match velocities with Earth as it sped by, or try to catch Lehaim after that, several months later. Of course, the King would have sent angels to help, if that had ever happened, but it never did. People in this age did not make mistakes any longer. Living with King Jesus had made them all perfectionists, except that everyone really did everything perfectly, these days! (Computers were still used, but everyone could do perfect math in his own head, no matter how complex. It was not even taught in school any longer, since everyone born into this age, or resurrected into it, could already do flawless complex math at birth, or upon resurrection. The same gifts were present in language skills. Newborns could speak clearly, but did not yet know what all the words meant, until they learned!)

Anyway, people had also learned better engineering principles, and every yacht was also equipped with a small VASIMR rocket setup as emergency backup, in case of sail damage, or any other need for instant acceleration. It most likely could not take them all the way out to Jupiter, and back, but it could easily get them back to any one of the three main planets, in a few days, max.

King Jesus went on talking to them, as He calmly dismounted from Tzedek-Sus, and stood there with the horse, in mid air, just as though upon solid rock, and the horse stood with his mighty wings folded quietly away, watching King Jesus, just like everyone, and listening, and nodding his majestic horse head, every once in a while, when agreement with a good point was appropriate. (It was sort of like a horse version of "Amen!")

As He fed sugar cubes to His horse, King Jesus continued, " Okay, so this is a very, very special Jubilee next year, since we will have a Grand Jubilee every 1,000 years, from now on, forever, but there will always be only one First Grand Jubilee, and this is that one!"

"Instead of showing you a whole bunch of new, fantastic inventions, developments, constructions, or any other such things, I want to give you a very brief preview of what you will see next year, Jubilee 20, Grand Jubilee One, when, at high noon, on Yom Kippur, Gabriel sounds his shofar again, and I proclaim the Grand Jubilee!"

As soon as He said this, the sky was vividly filled with an intense, exquisitely, finely-detailed view of a huge, brilliant, glowing golden city, a mighty, walled city, as large as a small continent, with white-peaked mountains, and great, vast green forests, and huge patches of dense jungle, and enormous, deep blue lakes, and four great, white, noisy, rushing rivers, each one charging from the middle of the unimaginably long walls, each 216-foot tall wall also running, straight as a laser, for 1,377 miles, so that the rivers each emerged at about the 689 mile half-way point gate, one gate of twelve, each gate made of a single pearl, and guarded by a giant angel, and each pearl was over 200 feet in diameter, and the giant angels were even much taller. They each towered over the gates which they were assigned to watch.

The huge, nation-sized city was almost two million square miles, all within the great city walls, which were solid slabs of diamond, 216 feet tall by 1,377 miles long. The whole square monster of a city was entirely enclosed by this wall, a solid, one-piece diamond, 216 feet tall, and with a total length of 5,508 miles. The twelve holes for the gates had been made especially into the giant, one-piece diamond fence, and the giant pearls had been fused onto them. There were mountain ranges within the city, and some desert areas also, but not large ones. The tallest mountain in the city was Mount Moriah, which was perched, in its' proper place, along with all of the rest of old Jerusalem, at the very pinnacle of the city, on the far western side, right over the place where the original Temple had been built, by Solomon. Every stone in the old city had been changed into solid, purest gold, so free from all impurities, that it was transparent, like glass. It was actually not completely optically clear, but was more like the old glass bricks used in decorative walls during the middle 20th century. The difference was that it was solid gold, and one could somehow tell it, just by looking, even though no one had ever seen gold that pure before, anywhere in the universe.

The "camera" did a quick zoom, pan and flyby of all of the unusual highlights of New Jerusalem, and then the picture winked out, like a light! All of the people moaned and whined like disappointed little children, when that happened, with comments, of "Oh, no!" and "Come on!" and "Wait! Just one more minute, please!"

King Jesus smiled at them, and their mood lifted instantly, as when the sunlight burns through the depressing gray clouds, and He said, "Now, now! Just be cleared out before Yom Kippur, next year, all the way out of Egypt, too, and the whole Arabian Peninsula, too, as well as all of Turkey, and all of Iraq, and Iran. Stay out of the waters around there, too, including the Persian Gulf. I am going to bring New Jerusalem down to Earth, that Day, and you will all watch! This city has been built only by Me, and no other human hand has ever touched it, yet. This vision showed you the way it will be when I finally have finished it, a little over a year from now, and then, I will install it upon Earth, forever. My Temple, and My Capital City, will stand here, for all Eternity, as I have declared from ancient times. Behold, I make all things new!"

"Now, go home, celebrate this Sabbath Year, and then, do not tarry, but begin to move out of the whole region as soon as the second month of the Jubilee arrives, after you have quickly finished the usual Jubilee business. Do be vacant from here, but do be watching! Each of you will be able to find a place in the new city, once I have installed it here. Now, I bless you each, in the Name of the Father, the

Savior, and the Holy Spirit! Go home! SHALOM!"

As He finished, and vanished instantly, taking His great warhorse with Him, the people, still blinking from the glowing after-images in their minds, and eyes, began to turn, and find their ways home. They obeyed, and spent the next year, resting, and worshipping, and, when Year 1,000 began, they immediately started, worked through, and concluded the usual business which was required by the terms of the Jubilee. Then at the end of the first month of Jubilee, all of the people and animals living anywhere near the landing zone were moved out completely, taking with them anything that they wished to keep, except the buildings and roads. All of the people everywhere in the whole Solar System were ordered to make their ways back to the edges of the landing zone, before the Day of Atonement. Trains, and rocket ships, and planes, and helicopters, and hydrogen cars, and trucks, and, for those with strong enough wings to actually fly, even living wings, and also human feet, began the gathering of all people to witness the greatest spectacle which anyone would ever see, at least, since the overwhelming return of King Jesus!

At last, after long eons of waiting, the long-prophesied Day came, and everyone was eagerly waiting, watching, talking, and checking their cameras to be sure they got some good footage of the once-in-Eternity historic event. Folks were lined up all around the entire perimeter of the zone, which had been marked off with a bright stripe of orange paint at the very outer edge. Everyone stayed back a few feet from the actual stripe.

The noon hour arrived, and Gabriel, the only living person within the landing zone, appeared upon the Temple porch, raised his mighty shofar, and sent forth a note stronger than any note he had ever sounded in his whole life, and Gabriel was very ancient, indeed. The sound went out, through planets, and the whole Solar System, and out further still, to echo through the entire Universe. As the very long, powerful note faded in the distance, Gabriel quietly lowered the horn, placed it under his left arm, stretched his enormous wings, and quietly flew out of the landing zone.

Suddenly all living creatures heard King Jesus say, "SHALOM! I proclaim the First Grand Jubilee, to commemorate the First Thousand Years! Now, let all stand still, and see and hear the final mystery revealed!" As He finished saying this, suddenly everyone could see King Jesus high up in the air, seated upon His glorious Throne, out of which came voices, lightning, and thundering. The people were stunned, as always, to behold Him in His great glory!

As everyone watched and listened, fascinated, King Jesus raised His Royal Scepter, which was like a solid, white-hot rod of molten iron, with a strange jewel made entirely out of living light, having the shape of a three-dimensional Star of David, and He commanded, "Now come down here, City of the King! Take your rightful place upon My Earth, and dwell with us forever, right here!"

As He finished saying this, He began to slowly lower His right arm, holding the magnificent scepter, and a mighty thing in the sky, so grand in scale that a human mind could not quite grasp the size of it, especially when seen from ground level, began to obediently descend from Heaven, gracefully floating down like a feather toward the ground!

The people watching were gasping for breath, their hearts racing like never before, and everyone cheering and dancing, wild with excitement and joy. One little boy's puppy got so carried away with all of the excitement, that he frolicked and bounced his excited little body across the line, into the landing zone! The boy suddenly saw him, and yelled "Wait!" as he raced toward his puppy, which the puppy thought was still another game of chase, and the puppy headed still further away into the landing zone! The boy's father raced after him, saying a silent prayer, which Jesus heard, and King Jesus sent a mental command to one of the millions of angels escorting the City down to Earth, and that angel, along with a dozen more of his own angel buddies, streaked down and grabbed up the puppy, the little boy, and his father, and carried them out of the zone, as the overwhelming, monster-sized City floated steadily lower!

(Everyone watching this gave God thanks, and also thanked the angels, but the angels laughed, and made light of it, so that everyone would not be distracted by that event, and miss the great moment.)

As the people all stood watching, their faces were being chilled by a cold wind, which was being produced by the descent of the City. As it descended, it pushed all of the air out from under itself, and most of that air was from higher elevations, and air is cold, several thousand feet up. The sound they heard was a low, deep moan, as the wind sometimes does on strange nights. Everyone was staring open mouthed, as the great thing came closer, and the magnitude of it overcame their senses again. The angels stood beside them, and the one that had grabbed the little boy stood with one hand on his shoulder, making sure he did not wander off, again. In the other hand, he held the puppy, which was well-behaved, except that once in a while he tried to lick the angel's cheek!

The boy looked up at the huge angel beside him, and said, "What's your name?"

The mighty warrior smiled warmly back at the boy, knelt down to look him right in the eye, and said, "I am called Tzedek-el."

The rest of their conversation had to wait, since the City was now only about 100 feet up, and still lowering. The rate of descent slowed even more, but continued, until the landing was achieved, with a gentle thump, and a very slight shake, just one little time, through the ground they were standing upon, all around the 216-foot tall diamond wall.

Every detail which had been shown a year and a half earlier was precisely the way it had seemed in the vision. The City was majestic, in a way and scale which had never even been imagined before. The tallest peak in New Jerusalem was the Temple Mount, which towered three miles high over everything else. The whole Temple, mountain and all, and also the Mount of Olives, as well as the entire city of old Jerusalem, now sat atop the pinnacle of the Holy Mountain, with snow all around the old city limits, but not allowed to touch the old city or the Temple. The good Lord wanted all of His pure gold buildings to shine with glory, not snow. The whole mountain, and almost the whole interior of the whole nation-scale City was covered with green, growing plants, including every kind of tree, bush, vine, grain field, and flower, and even a few of the weeds, which the good Lord also considered a type of flower, too, although He would never again allow them to trouble His Garden! Large blue lakes were just waiting for swimming and skiing. Roads were already built and ready, and everything was fully stocked and prepared. There were large estates, small cottages, even campgrounds everywhere, and the whole place was like a giant, beautiful park. The plants here were not neatly trimmed or shaped, because the Lord grew all of the plants, however He chose to shape them. No two plants were identical, but each was unique, as with the good Lord's snowflakes. The overall impression was still one of absolute perfection, and trimming the plants would have ruined them.

The whole visual and emotional impact produced in the observers was quite astonishing, with many people crying, even if they never usually did, and even the most sour personalities were laughing, singing, and shouting praise and thanks to God! For the first time ever, in all of the history of Creation, all, every one, of the mighty angels, stood speechless beside the humans, and the angels actually began to quietly weep, with huge, happy smiles upon their faces, as they shed tears of purest joy, for the glory of King Jesus, and for the final prophecies becoming fulfilled, even this very Day of Days, right before their tear-filled eyes!

The spectacle of New Jerusalem was so vast and overwhelming that many fell down in stunned amazement. They sat there on the dirt, unable to function, until the shock wore off a bit. Nobody had been hurt, not even a scratch, although for a few minutes it had been close, with the puppy and all of that.

The wonder and marvel was without ceasing, and, as people began to calm down, and shake off the numbness of the shock, more comments were being made, like "Wow!" and "Glory to God, in the highest, and now, on Earth, too!" and "Far out, Man!" from the California Christians.

The terrain was something special, as the good Lord had seen fit to precisely duplicate certain things of wonder from throughout the whole Earth, such as; He cloned all of Yosemite Valley, including El Capitan, Half-Dome, and all the rest inside the City walls. The original landscape was not touched, just duplicated very precisely. He had some of the Norwegian fjords, the Grand Canyon, Lake Tahoe, Crater Lake,

Thousand Island Lake, the Sequoias and giant redwoods, from the American West Coast, and many other scenic wonders from all over the world. People never had to leave the City, if they wanted to go on a scenic adventure!

Even though Mount Moriah and the Temple were the highest points in the City, there were several other mountain ranges, as well. The best of the Swiss Alps had also been duplicated, as had also the Grand Teton Range. Included also inside the walls of the City was the original Mountain of Moses, in ancient Midian, located in the northwest region of the Arabian Peninsula. Jabel-el-Laws had always been a huge part of God's history with mankind, and now, it was going to be honored as it always should have been. It still wore the burned black mark all over the top half of it, from the Day when the Lord had descended to the mountain, and then, He had given the Law to Moses.

Even so, without question, the most beautiful mountain that ever had existed, Mount Moriah, was now standing right there, solid, real, and right in front of them. It was impossible to look away, for more than a few seconds, and then, the eyes and mind were magnetically latched back upon the Holy Mountain. One other of the most important four mountains that ever existed was also still in its' place, holding Hebron up in the air. Mount Hebron had been where the whole Hebrew culture had started, and the tomb of Joseph was still there, where he had ordered the children of Israel to carry up, and bury his bones, after they left Egypt. Most people never knew that the tomb of Noah had also been there, from shortly after the flood.

Perhaps the fourth most important mountain ever was also within the City limits, also where it originally stood. Mount Ararat had hidden the wreckage of the Ark, until the Day King Jesus had returned, and now, the Ark had been fully rebuilt, and restored, and mounted securely upon Mount Ararat, just where it had initially come to rest, as a wonder and a memorial for all generations, to remind us of God's mercy and power.

The people stared for hours, as the angels flew into the City, to make final opening day arrangements, and then, at the ninth hour, the hour of prayer, King Jesus appeared on Tzedek-Sus, right over the Temple, and shouted, "SHALOM! Come into My City, and let My House be filled! Come, and explore, and taste the wonders made ready for you, since before the world began! Those whose names were read last of all in the Book of Life may enter first, and choose your homes, unless you are one of the folks for which we have special reservations, which we will tell you as you enter the gates. A few of you I will always want to have living very near to My House, but all good people will be welcome, somewhere in this new City of Love!"

Then He shouted, "Behold My new Temple!" People's eyes obediently snapped to the very peak of Mount Moriah, and they saw the solid, translucent gold wonder, the original temple, as designed by God, and built by Solomon! It gleamed with its' own internal golden light, and all about the Temple was a bright rainbow, completely encasing it in vivid colored light, and the aura of the light seemed to be shaped like a giant gemstone, resembling an emerald!

The great roof of the Temple opened up, and people could see the interior, and King Jesus was suddenly seated upon His Throne of glory, and a rushing torrent of noisy white water rushed out from the base of the Throne, and out the front door of the Temple, and then split, and split again, with one branch heading East, one going West, one going North, and one going South. The Living Water in these streams increased astonishingly rapidly, by geometric progression, as though the water were making more water to flow along with it, which it actually was doing! By the time the flow had reached the edge of the pinnacle mesa, four mighty rivers of living water leaped over the edges into the air, and cascaded down the sides of Mount Moriah, making the four most beautiful waterfalls ever seen, with great roaring torrents, hurtling down from a three-mile tall cliff! The rivers splashed into huge basin pools at the bottom of the mountain, and then, roared out of the central gate in each of the four mighty walls, and then dispersed living water all over the planet, being named the North Jordan, the East Jordan, the West Jordan, and the South Jordan.

Right in front of the Temple door, with its' behemoth sized roots straddling the River of Life (as it exited the Temple, and still had not yet split) there stood the giant Tree of Life. It stood so tall that its' tip top leaves were the same precise height as the Temple roof. Its' branches stretched out wide over almost the entire old city area. It bore twelve different kinds of fruit, one per month, and its' leaves could heal any disease, or sickness, or injury. True, in this age, such things were very rare, and always the result of accidents, but they still happened once in a while, to the very young, which were not yet in their full immortal strength. The whole Tree, and its' leaves, and its' fruit, glowed and shimmered with internal light, and it flashed iridescent colors like a chameleon, all over its' bark and roots. The glow from it was always so bright, that one could read from that light!

Standing down outside, at ground level, the people could only see the very tallest things in the City. The diamond wall was 216 feet tall, and the lowest parts of it were twelve foundation slabs, each made from one giant jewel. First in the list was diamond, and then came eleven others, including ruby, emerald, sapphire, and so on. On each slab of gemstone, the name of one of the twelve Apostles was engraved deep into the stone, and the letters of the names glowed with a light of their own! These slabs kept the entire structure of the City very solid and stable, forever.

As the people stared in wonder, overcome by awe, they all saw and heard King Jesus say, "Well, I told you that I was going to do precisely this, eventually. I know it seemed to take forever, more for Me, than for you! Nonetheless, it is done, and I have now proven to you all that I am indeed a Man of My Word!"

"BEHOLD, I MAKE ALL THINGS NEW!"

WOLVES BACK IN THE GARDEN

It was about 5:30 in the morning. The sky had never quite grown completely dark this wonderful night, but it had remained a little brighter than a full moon night, with the sky itself never fully turning black, but a very, very dark, deep shade of blue, instead. The moon and stars were still quite visible, especially since yesterday's Yom Kippur Festival had been just three days before the full moon.

Adam rolled over and sat up, swinging his feet to the floor of the tree house, and, standing fluidly up, walked to the window, where he saw that his own personal living dream had come true. Down below, in the wide fields, he saw his wife, Queen Eve, walking with their two wolves, as she was already out and about, picking their fresh breakfast.

In the strange, early, not-yet-dawn light, Eve could have seemed a ghost, but Adam knew that she was very real, and very much alive. She was the most beautiful woman that God had ever made, and she still remained the flawless original of womanly perfection that He had created.

Everyone had celebrated their heads off yesterday, and most of last night, and the music and dancing were still going on this morning, over there in the mega-city of New Jerusalem. They had been there along with everyone else, for the landing of the City, but had returned to their tree house in the Garden, as evening had arrived. The Garden of Eden was once again established and running, fully operational, right where it had started. The lowering of the world's ocean levels had once more opened up the north eastern arm of the Red Sea, which was the Gulf of Aquba. The sheer walls of the great cliffs all around the boundaries of

Eden kept would-be tourists out, since Eden was still considered a very holy place unto the Lord, and He was very exclusive about just which people that He let enter there. For the most part, it was reserved for the original people and animals that were there in the beginning, right up until the time that the worm messed things up. These days, there were no serpents in Eden.

So, down there in the deep basin, (hidden for the time between the Garden, and the Return, and long buried under seawater) were plants, of every kind, and animals, of every kind, except serpents, and all lived and thrived, just as the good Lord had meant for them all along. They had all been resurrected, and would not die anymore, but the Lord kept the birth rate very low, so that Eden would not be overrun with newborns.

The only plants which were not there were the Tree of Life, which now grew in front of the Temple, up in the Holy City,

and the Tree of Knowledge, which had
been changed, genetically, by King Jesus,
so that it could no longer contain or
impart the knowledge of evil, forever. It
still gave knowledge, but now, only the
knowledge of Good. The Tree of
Knowledge was therefore not in front of
the Temple, but in front of the main hall
of the new University of Israel, which
was the world's largest and very finest
learning institution! It was located at the
base of the three-mile-tall Mount Moriah,
so that people could drive in and out
easier, for all the college football games,
and so forth.

Adam slid down the tree trunk silently,
and went over to the "barn" clearing,
where the cows were already up and
milling around, waiting for him to come
milk them. He usually woke up closer to
4:00, or 4:30, but last night had been a
big party for all of them. He greeted the
cows, milked them, and then he headed
over to the chickens, to see if any of them

wanted to share some eggs with them this morning. Once he had some eggs, and had thanked the chickens, as he had the cows, he headed back to their kitchen area. As he arrived around the bend, Wolf and She-wolf came bouncing up to greet him, wagging their whole bodies, somehow, just like they always did, whenever he came near them. Eve saw him, and dropped what she was holding, and ran around the table to grab his neck, covering his cheeks with kisses, and giggles! All the time, the wolves were barking like puppies, and licking his toes and ankles, driving him crazy with tickles!

Unable to play it straight any longer, Adam burst out laughing, and shoved them all just a couple of inches away and said, "Man, oh man! What in the world got into all of you, today?" They were all usually very affectionate to him, but this was extreme, even for them.

Eve laughed, a little sly laugh, with twinkling eyes, and said, "Let's just say, for now, that I had a very interesting dream, last night."

Adam groaned, and said with a wry smile, "Oh, no!"

Eve laughed out loud, and poked him hard in the ribs, so hard that he grunted in surprise, and she said, "All right, just for that, eat your breakfast, smarty-wings, and now, I'm not gonna tell you anything else for a hint!"

Adam chuckled, as he sat down obediently, and, when all of them were settled, he bowed his noble head, and said thanks to the good Lord. Then they ate. The food was perfect, of course, but the company was better, still.

After they were done, Adam stood up, and said, "Thanks, Honey! That was great, especially those fresh-baked biscuits, with fresh butter and honey. The Lord sure does feed us very well!"

He looked across the clearing, to the path leading into the woods where he had met with the good Lord every morning, back in the morning of the Creation. They had not done that anymore since the sin of mankind, and Adam missed their One-on-one personal meetings every morning, especially the ones on Saturday mornings. He said, "I'll be back in a little bit." Eve did not answer, because she knew precisely what he was thinking, and she wanted to let him continue in his pathways of thought, undisturbed. She watched, as he turned, and walked toward the path entrance. Wolf was right there along with him, since Adam could go nowhere on Earth, except when ordered, without Wolf with him!

Adam was deep in thought, as they walked along the forest path, heading for the little spot that the good Lord had set aside for them. Wolf ventured a small-talk type comment, and said, "Momma looks a lot better, now that she has her wings back!"

Adam suddenly stopped, turned, kneeled down, looked Wolf straight in the eyes, and said, "Yes, Wolf. Please, we hope, and ask, that you, and She-wolf, and all of the other animals will forgive us, for causing all of that mess." As he finished the sentence, Adam suddenly could not look into Wolf's eyes any more, and he lowered his face, and a tear fell from each perfect eye to the ground. Wolf immediately leaped up into his face, tongue licking frantically, as he tried to comfort and re-assure Adam that there was nothing to forgive, even though they both remembered differently. Adam hugged his great, furry, mighty-muscled neck, and said, "Well, thank you, fur-Brother! I can actually promise you that such a thing will never happen again!"

As they came out the end of the little path, a huge surprise awaited them, and Adam fell instantly to his knees, then his face, as his eyes suddenly were filled with the radiant glory of King Jesus!

Jesus stepped over to him, lifted him up, smiled, and said, "Shalom, Adam!"

Adam stammered, "Shalom, my Lord!"

Jesus said, "I have missed our meetings, also, but things have been a bit hectic, for these last thousand years, or so. Now, since the new City is landed, and things are completed, I can take time to do the things which I have missed doing, for all this time!"

King Jesus looked over at Wolf, and smiled, and said, "Good boy, Wolf! I am very proud of you, and all of your descendants. You all stood beside My little brothers, and sisters, in times of joy, and sorrow, and peace, and war, and pleasure, and pain, and life, and death, and therefore, you, and all of yours, will have great honor, forever!" As He finished, He tossed Wolf a bone, just as juicy and flavorful as a real, hunted-down-and-killed bone would have been, even though this was a cloned one. Wolf expertly caught it in his teeth, and cracked through it in one chomp! He then sat down to nibble the chunks, swallowing a lot of them whole. As Adam and the good Lord spoke quietly, for the next ten minutes, the pieces of the cow's thighbone completely disappeared, becoming one with the Wolf. All of the wolves in the world now resembled Wolf and She-wolf, in their new glory, since the Lord had made them huge, and had given them wings, and had made them to glow with their own light, as men and women now did, also. God is living light, and, those creatures, which He had reserved for Eternity, and who had willingly served Him well, in times of war, would always now glow with their own lights, from the re-born spirits within them. No one made or sold flashlights, candles, or batteries for such things any longer. No one needed them, when everyone sort of radiated a soft (or intense, as needed) green light. Some folks glowed more red, some glowed more blue, some glowed more amber, or gold, and some, purest white, but everyone had their own special, unique set of colors and lights all over them and within them, as individual as fingerprints! Human eyes, like those of the good Lord Himself, could burn like lasers, if need arose for that, also.

One more bit of special honor was this: many special creatures, on an individual basis, of personal reward, including some men, women, children, wolves, horses, and many others, which had served well, now also had functioning wings, and now, even more of them had this, since yesterday's change and fulfillment.

As Adam and the good Lord finished their morning meeting, the Lord blessed them, bid them farewell, and then vanished. Adam and Wolf trotted back home, greeted the girls, drank a lot of water, and then, Adam said, "Well, He was there! Was that your dream?"

Eve smiled, again with that sly little smile, which she had also had since the first Garden, and said, "Yes, that was a part of it!"

He shook his head, as he grabbed a small sack of the special Velcro-type flower blossoms which he and Wolf used in their games of chase and tag, when they played with the wild horses. "Woman, what am I gonna do with you, anyway?"

She laughed, a note of pure musical delight, as was everything else about her, at least as far as Adam felt. She answered him, "Well, we can discuss more about that, later this evening, but for this morning, we are declaring this Ladies' Day at the horse-tag games!"

As soon as she said this, She-wolf came bouncing around the tree trunk, and she carried in her mouth another of the small bags, filled with Velcro-blossoms!

Eve gave a shout of joy, and she, and She-wolf ran out of the kitchen toward the great meadow where the boys always played! Adam and Wolf were right behind them, and the race was on, and these characters all had functioning wings, too, so it was a mixed cross-country scramble, under trees on foot, then leap back into the air, once clear, then back to ground, and sprint under more tree limbs, until they finally arrived, not even winded, but each of them laughing hysterically, since Eve had actually beaten Adam by a couple of split seconds, but she had done it by tripping him, at the last few steps, and he fell into the dust with a loud crash, and stood up laughing like a kid at recess! "You cheated!" he shouted.

Eve giggled back at him, almost unable to speak for the mirth of it all, and between laughs, managed to say, "You've known me all this time, and you expected less?"

All four of them collapsed in a heap of good natured wrestling and tickling, and licking, from the wolves, and tail-wagging, also from the wolves, until, a few seconds later, they all heard the deep voice of their friend Horse say, "So, are you guys gonna just roll around in the dust all day, or do you want us to humiliate your slow little legs?"

They all jumped up, brushing off dust, and smiled to see the dozen or so horses that had been their close friends from ancient times!

Adam said, "Okay, everyone knows the rules! Come over here and let us put on the Velcro-blossoms, and let the games begin!"

A few minutes later, the great meadow exploded with wild streaks of living missiles, as some of the fastest creatures with flesh bodies that were ever created began a high-speed chase. The games continued for over an hour, until they were all gasping for breath, and the team of Adam and Wolf was ahead by only one blossom! They all stopped for a few minutes for water break, and then, while they were attaching new Velcro blossoms to the flanks of the horses, to begin another round, before lunch, they all heard a distinctive Voice behind them, and instantly dropped to their knees, humans, wolves, and horses alike.

The Voice had asked calmly, "Can anybody play?"

As they turned to look, they all saw King Jesus standing there, and beside Him also stood His great horse, Tzedek-Sus! The excitement level rose dramatically!

Adam said, "Of course, Lord, and, of course, You already know all of the rules. Whose team will You be joining?"

King Jesus laughed, and replied, "While I am, and always will be, on your side, Tzedek-Sus and I will form our own team, and we will even leave you with the twenty or so blossom lead, which you each already have!"

King Jesus turned, stuck a brightly glowing, golden Velcro blossom upon the flank of Tzedek-Sus, and said, "Go!"

Everyone erupted instantly into blurs and streaks of motion, but the rules required all activity to be at ground level, so all wings were being kept tightly folded. After two more hours, as lunch time was near, King Jesus and Tzedek-Sus had drawn even with Adam for the lead, and no one else had been able to score any points since He had joined the game. He was just way too fast and strong, even just using His Own natural physical strength, grown mighty over decades of lumberjack-type carpentry, and also a lifetime hobby of climbing mountains without any safety gear. (He always had known that the angels would bear Him up in hands, lest He dash His foot against a stone!)

Among the horses, Tzedek-Sus truly was their king, and none of them could evade the snapping teeth of Wolf and She-wolf nearly as well. Adam and Eve could not lay a hand on him, either.

King Jesus said, "Okay, one more point, and then lunch!" As He said this, He grabbed Eve's arm, and instantly pushed it over to the golden blossom upon the flank of Tzedek-Sus, and sort of wrapped her surprised hand around the blossom, so she caught it, and drew even in score with Adam, and Himself, so the match ended in a three-way tie!

Eve laughed delightedly, and so did Adam, as did the wolves and horses, in their own style of laughter!

As they began to turn to go back to the tree house, to eat lunch, they asked the good Lord if He had time to stay for lunch, but He said that He would be back in a few days, but had much business to tend this day. They thanked Him, and just before He went, He looked at all of the horses, and said, "Now, I want all of you to know how My Own horse feels!"

The second He said this, all of the horses suddenly had new, strong wings, and they began to flap and stretch them in amazed delight! He went on, "Now, I have to go back to the City, but Tzedek-Sus will stay here with you this month, and teach all of you how to actually use those mighty wings! After this, each of you will teach all of the other horses in this world, and also upon the other worlds, how to use and enjoy their new wings, also, which I will give them next month, when you are ready to train them."

Then He turned to His Own horse, and said, "As for you, and your donkey-kinfolk, which have endured and overcome such things as even the horses never had to suffer, well, I have something for you all, as well!"

Suddenly, standing near Tzedek-Sus was a small gray donkey, and the horses all whinnied as soon as they saw him, and shouted out "Donkey!" Tzedek-Sus ran up to him, and began to nuzzle his gray donkey neck, saying, "Grandfather! I have missed you!" The little gray donkey was suddenly surrounded by all of them, and it was made clear to him that every one of them knew him, remembered him, and still loved him, too!

After a few minutes, they heard King Jesus quietly clear His throat, and they all turned to look at Him. He said, "Now, I wish to give, to all of the donkeys, a special gift, for all of their tough, humble, faithful service, as they carried kings and prophets, and also Me, before I was born, and then, into Egypt after that, and Tzedek-Sus was still a little gray donkey the Day that we stormed the stronghold of the devil. Now, be blessed, indeed, all you wonderful donkeys!"

When He said this, Donkey began to grow, and glow, and sprouted wings, and became exceedingly mighty and beautiful, becoming almost identical to Tzedek-Sus! They each had a brilliant, glowing, golden cross upon their backs, made right into the fur, running lengthwise down between the wings! In the old world, those crosses had been charcoal grey, but all true donkeys related to Donkey had worn them, in honor of the Day of War, when Tzedek-Sus had carried King Jesus into battle, back in ancient Jerusalem. Somehow, they all knew that every donkey, in all of the worlds, had just been blessed the very same Way!

Donkey threw back his now-majestic head and screamed a victory scream, the war-cry of overwhelming faith, at last fulfilled! He turned to thank King Jesus, and said, "Thank You, Lord! I will try to be worthy!"

King Jesus also threw back His majestic Head, and laughed a happy laugh, shaking the whole world with joy, and He said, "Little Friend, you were always worthy!"

King Jesus stretched out His Own mighty wings, looked toward the City, and said, "I will see you all here a week from today, and see how your training is going. Have fun, and try not to fly into each other! Shalom!"

They all watched Him streak away into the sky, trailing dazzling tracers behind Him. Ten thousand angels flew into formation behind Him, just because they liked being near Him.

As they faded from view, the humans and wolves turned to head home. Adam chuckled, and asked, "Well, what was the rest of your dream, Honey?"

Eve laughed her wonderful musical laugh, and shook her beautiful, long hair out of her face, and then smiled at him, like another sunrise, and said, softly, "I dreamed that today our King would visit, yes, and He did. I also dreamed that He told me that today, He would make sure that I got to win, too, and that I would never be a loser, again!"

ABOUT THE AUTHOR

I was raised by wonderful Christian parents, people that loved our good Lord, and introduced me to Him, as soon as I could grasp the idea of God.

I love things of the Spirit, and also things of science. One God, and one Reality. The same God which made the angels also made test tubes. There is only One Maker, and only one Reality. People need to understand the truth of that concept. That driving principle has kept me working upon these books, to try to illustrate that God is God, and that God is good. I hope I have made that point abundantly, but, still, I encourage each person to study God's Word, and see if these things may be correct! Open your heart and mind, humbly seek the truth, follow the evidence, and see what you may discover.

(Remember, Scripture is Truth, but my writings are fiction, based upon Truth.)

WOULD KING JESUS HAVE A SPACE PROGRAM?

The time is after the return of King Jesus. Things are being rebuilt, cleaned up, and made new. What adventures await the Son of God, and the rest of the human race?

The first Universal event horizon occurred when God, as Father, said, "BE LIGHT!" The light still shines!

The second Universal event horizon occurred when God, as Savior, raised His Own body from death. He is still alive!

The third Universal event horizon will occur when New Jerusalem is lowered from Heaven to Earth, and God, as Father/ Savior/ Holy Spirit arrives, in Person, with New Jerusalem, and makes His permanent, Eternal home among the children of man!

What might that look like? Look, and see!

www.ingramcontent.com/pod-product-compliance
Lightning Source LLC
Chambersburg PA
CBHW052028020726
47501CB00004B/1307